W9-CFB-719

SILENT
CATHEDRALS

SILENT
CATHEDRALS

•

Sandra Dark

AVALON BOOKS
NEW YORK

Woonsocket Harris Public Library

© Copyright 2004 by Sandra Dark
Library of Congress Catalog Card Number: 2004091851
ISBN 0-8034-9672-9
All rights reserved.
All the characters in this book are fictitious,
and any resemblance to actual persons,
living or dead, is purely coincidental.
Published by Thomas Bouregy & Co., Inc.
160 Madison Avenue, New York, NY 10016

PRINTED IN THE UNITED STATES OF AMERICA
ON ACID-FREE PAPER
BY HADDON CRAFTSMEN, BLOOMSBURG, PENNSYLVANIA

01/20/05

To Wayne and Merrie Elisens—
for friendship and inspiration.

D

13.80

9.9.04

T. BOUREGY

Prologue

"Oh, no. Not again!"

Perched twelve feet high on the crossbeam of the rope-netting climb at the end of the obstacle course, Kate O'Riley squinted up at the gunmetal-gray clouds pouring over the mountaintop.

She quickly hammered a final brad flush with the beam and scrambled down the heavy rope netting. Just as she reached the ground, a bolt of lightning seemed to explode directly overhead. Kate cried out and took off running down the hiking trail toward the Camp Reliant compound.

The clouds opened and the wind picked up, lashing ice-cold raindrops against her bare legs. Frantic to reach cover, she veered right at a fork in the trail, taking a shortcut to a deep outcropping marking the entrance to an uncharted cave system just outside Camp Reliant's property line.

Kate lunged beneath the protective overhang and fell against the limestone wall of the cave entrance, gasping for breath, soaked to the skin, and seething with frustra-

1

tion. She had a lot riding on her first season as a camp counselor. But the current six-week program had been rained on nearly every day, disrupting the July timetable and severely challenging Kate's work with troubled kids.

Especially where one Zach Forrest was concerned.

She flipped her wheat-blond braid over her shoulder and squeezed the rainwater from it. Camp Reliant was just over the mountain from the affluent resort of White Sulphur Springs, West Virginia. But as she peered out at the storm-tossed trees outside the cave, she knew she wasn't within shouting distance of the nearest human being.

Kate wasn't particularly disturbed by her isolation. Like many of her students, she had spent much of her childhood as a loner. But that was before Camp Reliant worked its magic on her ten years ago. Now she had returned, in hopes of paying back the priceless gift that she had been given as a child. If the weather would just let her.

A spray of rain blew under the overhang, followed by another splintering crack of thunder. Kate took a step deeper into the cave—and heard voices behind her.

Voices?

She peered into the black depths of the cave. "Is anybody there?"

Another deafening boom of thunder drowned out her words. Lightning flashes were coming almost on top of each other now, and distressingly close.

A hollow burst of laughter echoed from the cave. With a gasp, she backpedaled toward the rain-swept entrance as a yellowish shape lunged toward her out of the darkness. Kate shrieked, closed her eyes, and took a wild swing with one arm.

To her surprise, her fist connected with something

solid just as an ear-splitting crash of thunder shattered the air around her. She leaped back against the rough limestone wall as her would-be attacker gave a loud grunt and hit the ground at her feet.

He didn't move. Kate did. Without so much as a backward glance, she turned and bolted out into the storm, unable to halt her headlong flight toward camp.

Chapter One

A fitful breeze rustled through the tree canopy on the side of the mountain. The sharp, sweet smell of damp pine needles filled the air as Kate followed Cliff Peet up the trail toward the cave entrance that she had fled just an hour earlier.

"Katie, you oughta go on back to camp now," Peet said for the umpteenth time. "Let me look into this."

"I want to see for myself, Mr. Peet." She eyed the back of her employer's bald head. He was barely two inches taller than Kate, and nearly three times her age—a stocky wedge of solid muscle. Despite his pronounced limp, he could out-hike any counselor in Camp Reliant. She felt totally safe in his company. "Maybe it was just my imagination."

Peet barked a humorless laugh. "Not unless you punched a tree, it wasn't."

Kate flexed her bruised and swollen right hand. Now that the storm had passed and she had changed into dry clothes, the entire incident seemed unreal.

They rounded a bend in the trail. The cave loomed

ahead, a freshly lightning-blasted hickory tree just to the left of the entrance. Kate hung back only slightly as her boss marched up the stony incline to the entrance and peered inside.

"Huh. Looky here." He reached down and picked up a bowl-shaped mirrored object attached to a black elastic band. "It's a lantern used by spelunkers."

"Used by what?"

"Cave explorers," he explained. Demonstrating, he stretched the band around his head so the bowl settled on his forehead. "This fits on a hardhat. Puts out quite a bit of light for such a little thing." He whipped it off and fingered the center of the bowl. "The carbide element has been busted out." He examined the ground again. "The dirt's pretty scuffed up. Looks like whoever left this lantern is long gone."

That was good news to Kate as they moved back out into the sunlight.

"You know, this cave isn't on Camp Reliant property," Peet said. "But I'm gonna see about getting this entrance sealed up anyway, just to be on the safe side."

Kate nodded. As the camp's owner and director, Cliff Peet's first concern was always with safety. Most of the kids came to view the crusty former Army sergeant as a grandfather figure. So did Kate.

Peet turned and headed back down the trail toward camp. Kate trotted to catch up.

Just before they rounded the bend in the trail, she glanced back toward the cave, wondering about the man she had walloped. Guilt curled into a tight knot in the pit of her stomach. Maybe the poor guy hadn't meant to attack her after all.

That possibility troubled her mightily.

* * *

In a clearing at the foot of the hiking trail, two low cabins served as dormitories for Camp Reliant's students, one for girls, and one for boys. Across the clearing stood the dining hall. Next to that rose the big two-story main cabin, Cliff Peet's quarters occupying the entire top floor. Kate and Camp Reliant's other two counselors, one of them Peet's own daughter, shared the ground floor with the kitchen and laundry room.

At the head of the clearing, a thin waterfall streamed down the steep mountainside. Nestled among the trees, the entire camp had a snug, homey look about it.

Kate found her group of eleven kids in the dining hall, each of the ten to twelve-year-olds rigged up with a small backpack, ready for the day's scheduled hike. Cliff Peet's nineteen-year-old daughter, Lana, was delivering a lecture on tree frogs. When Kate entered the cabin, Lana glanced up, looking at once relieved and irked.

"It's about time you got back," Lana said.

The girl's brittle tone unsettled Kate, but she let it pass. Ever since Kate hired on at Camp Reliant last May, she'd had a distinct impression that Lana was jealous of her. She figured that either Lana resented being just a junior counselor, or she saw Kate as a threat to her crush on senior counselor Toby Harris.

"All right kids." Kate clapped her hands. "Everybody outside to form up."

She stepped out of the way as her charges stampeded past. Lana didn't budge from the stool where she was perched.

"Where's Toby?" Kate asked.

Lana shrugged. "Cook sent him on an emergency run to the store for supplies."

"Oh." Kate frowned. "In that case, it looks like you're with me this afternoon."

"That's what I figured." Lana fluffed her kinky red hair and tugged at the hem of her tank top as she slouched down off the stool. Her passion for her work left a lot to be desired. She was taller than her father and totally lacked his upbeat attitude.

As Kate followed her outside, she couldn't help noticing the butterfly tattoo on the back of Lana's left shoulder. She had seen Cliff scowling at it a number of times, and knew father and daughter had had words over the new ornament.

The youngsters had lined up in the clearing. They wore bright orange Camp Reliant T-shirts and denim shorts, with whistles on leather lanyards that the kids had braided themselves. Kate smiled as she did her routine head-count. Ten faces grinned back.

She frowned, and counted again. The number came out the same. It took Kate a moment to figure out which child was missing. Her heart sank, but she wasn't surprised.

"Where's Zach?" she asked.

"What difference does it make?" asked Annie Rich, a frizzy-haired moppet. The rest of the group grumbled agreement.

Kate didn't like the way they were siding against one of their own. Zach Forrest had been a disciplinary problem from the first day, but Camp Reliant was all about learning teamwork. "Have we forgotten the camp slogan?" she asked.

Heads ducked in shame. Kate cleared her throat, waiting.

Finally, ten voices piped more or less in unison, "Strength in unity."

"Excellent. Now who can tell me where Zach is?"

Sandra Dark

With a long-suffering sigh, Annie pointed toward the boys' dormitory.

"Okay," Kate said. "Who wants to be Zach's trail buddy this afternoon?"

After a pause, "I guess I will," came a voice from the end of the line.

"Thank you, Tommy," Kate said, astonished.

Painfully shy, Tommy Reyes was the smallest, least athletic member of the group. He invariably brought up the rear in the trail hikes, and had yet to complete the obstacle course within the allotted time. But he fell in beside her as she headed across the clearing.

They climbed the hand-hewn wooden steps at the end of the boys' dorm and pulled open the door. Two rows of bunks lined the walls. Zach Forrest sat cross-legged on the last bunk on the right, hunched over a deck of cards, playing solitaire. Kate moved resolutely down the center of the aisle and stopped at the foot of his bunk.

She watched him for a moment, aware that he was a brilliant child. Someday he would turn into a handsome man with his shock of raven hair—though in her humble opinion, a twelve-year-old could do without a gold earring. The earring gave him the look of a student pirate, which very well might have been his intention.

As frustrating as Zach was, Kate couldn't help aching for him. Locked up inside his rebellious anger was a whole lot of pain. His downhill spiral had begun just a year ago with the loss of his father. She said, "Zach, your teammates are waiting."

"Big deal."

Kate took a slow, calming breath. According to the camp's rules, she couldn't order him to go. He had to make that decision for himself. "If that's your choice, then Tommy will have to miss the hike too. He's volunteered to be your trail buddy today."

"Please, Zach," Tommy pleaded. "I really, really want to go on the hike."

Pleased that Tommy had spoken up for himself so forcefully, Kate crossed her fingers behind her back and hoped the boy might sway Zach.

"I'm getting better at keeping up, Zach," Tommy added less firmly. "I promise not to hold you back on the trail."

Kate wanted to support Tommy, but let the boys work it out between themselves if they could. The more good choices they learned to make for themselves, the more they would take away from their stay at Camp Reliant.

Zach glowered at his cards, then angrily swept them off the quilt onto the floor. "Okay, okay!" He hopped off the bed, stalked down the aisle, and slammed out the door.

Tommy brightened, oblivious to Zach's show of temper.

Kate breathed a sigh of relief, taking Zach's choice not to let down his trail buddy as a good sign. But the afternoon was still young, and she harbored no illusions that Zach had turned over a completely new leaf. All she could do was hope for the best.

The afternoon had turned hot and steamy. Kate stopped along the leaf-mulched deer path and took a drink from her water bottle. Down along the steep trail, eleven kids copied her. Looking bored, Lana Peet brought up the rear, just behind Tommy and Zach. Kate holstered her water bottle and turned to lead the kids on up the mountain.

The hikers had almost made it to the top of the trail when

Kate spotted two men clad in bright-yellow coveralls headed toward them from above. Both wore backpacks, with ropes, hardhats, and other gear hanging from straps on the packs and from belts around their waists. The equipment jangled like wind chimes as they walked. Both men were as lean as whips, and moved along in a loose-limbed, effortless gait.

When the men caught sight of the group moving up the mountain toward them, they halted in their tracks. Kate watched them quietly exchange words as she approached at the head of her hiking party. The shorter of the two, who appeared to be no taller than her five-feet-four, suddenly burst out laughing. The taller man, mahogany-haired and wearing mirrored sunglasses, gave his companion a backhanded punch in the chest as if to shut him up.

"Afternoon, gentlemen," Kate called out, setting a friendly example for the kids. "Enjoying your hike?"

"Matter of fact, no," said the taller man in a deep voice that carried easily in the clear air. "But it's the only way to get to a cave system up there." He motioned higher up the mountain, in the direction of the cave where Kate had taken refuge from the storm earlier in the day. "This morning's rain caused a rock slide that blocked our shortcut. This is the long way around."

"Ah." Eyeing their yellow coveralls, Kate suddenly had an uneasy feeling about the men. Not fear. It was more like a sense of impending embarrassment. "You, uh, go there often?"

The shorter man grinned.

Without even looking at him, his companion punched him again and murmured, "Cut it out, Mark." Then he worked his jaw to one side as if suppressing a smile of his own, and said to Kate, "We've spent the better part of a week up there, surveying the caverns."

"You're surveyors?" Kate asked, growing more nervous by the second.

"I'm a geologist," he said. "Name's Gavin Buckley." He held out a hand.

Kate hesitated, and then extended her own hand. When his larger hand engulfed hers, she felt a confusing surge of excitement. He held on longer than necessary or even polite before releasing her.

In a tight voice, she said, "Kate O'Riley. We're all from Camp Reliant, down the hill."

"Mark Eisly," Gavin's friend said, and they went through the handshaking ritual again, this time without the lingering hold.

"You're a geologist too?" she asked.

"Hydrologist." When she gave him a quizzical look, he tilted his head toward his companion. "Gavin here studies rocks. I do water. Caverns have a lot of both."

"Ah," she said again, feeling stupid. She had never been inside a cavern, and knew next to nothing about them. She preferred fresh, open air with lots of clear, blue sky above.

Mark's grin had returned in force, and he kept shooting glances at his friend, as if waiting for him to do or say something. Gavin just stood there in the middle of the trail, his expression unreadable behind the mirrored sunglasses. But Kate had a feeling that he had been focused entirely on her almost since the moment they had first caught sight of each other.

After an awkward pause, Kate said, "Well, you guys have a good day."

She took a step to her right, intent on leading the group around the men. Gavin matched her move with a quick, catlike step to his left. Directly behind Kate, Annie Rich giggled.

Kate's confusion grew, along with that nagging sense that she was about to be buried beneath a stupendous avalanche of humiliation.

"Funny that we should run into each other like this," Gavin said. "Again."

"Again . . . ?" Kate's voice sounded strangled. She knew what was coming—knew, and wanted with all her heart to go hide behind a tree.

"That's right," Gavin drawled. He hooked one thumb over his belt, and with the other hand slowly removed his sunglasses. "Again."

"Oh!" was all she could get out.

Gavin Buckley had deep, warm, brown eyes, the kind that a girl could dive right into. At least, that description fit one of them. The other eye was swollen nearly shut, the surrounding flesh bearing a darkening bruise. He stood there twirling the sunglasses by one stem, watching Kate's reaction. She felt the color drain from her face.

"Back at the office," Mark said, turning to look at his partner's eye, "the general opinion is that it's the most impressive shiner that anyone has ever seen."

Kate's hand drifted up to clamp over her mouth, which seemed to be gaping wide. She could feel the kids crowding up close behind her to get a better look. Several of the boys offered varying expressions of admiration for the black eye. The girls mostly settled for a collective, "Ew-ee!"

Gavin kept his gaze riveted on Kate. After a moment, his lips stiffened into a hard line, perhaps to quell the twitch at the corners of his mouth.

Some time after that, Kate managed to lower her hand.

She threw back her shoulders and cleared her throat . . . twice. "Did you get that this morning?" she asked.

"Oh, yeah."

"At the cavern—" She pointed up the mountainside. "—over there?"

"You got it."

"During the storm?"

"Yup."

Kate looked down at her right hand. The knuckles were still red and a little puffy, but not near as bad as Gavin Buckley's eye. "Uh . . . I think there's been a, uh, misunderstanding."

"I've been wondering about that." He seemed to be enjoying her discomfort.

"I thought I was alone. I heard voices, then saw . . ." Kate offered him a sheepish smile. "I guess I got spooked."

"I guess. You were about to back right out into that electrical storm. Didn't anyone ever tell you how dangerous lightning is in the mountains?"

"Well, yes. But . . . I got spooked."

"You said that."

"Is that why you . . . ?"

"Ran into your fist?" He nodded once, slowly, and very gingerly replaced the sunglasses. But before it disappeared behind the mirrored lens, his good eye shone playfully. "Next time, I might think twice before trying to rescue a beautiful woman from the fury of Mother Nature."

Beautiful woman? Kate felt a flutter. "Oh, I am so sorry," she whispered, mortified.

"So am I, Kate O'Riley," he said. "At least you appear to have made it home safely."

"Yes." Though she had to admit that probably had been a miracle, considering the magnitude of the storm.

"Now if you'll kindly excuse us," he said with a slight bow, "Mark and I have to get back to work."

The two men continued on down the trail.

Kate turned to watch them leave, feeling that her apology had been grossly inadequate. After all, the geologist had been trying to save her life when she knocked him cold. He deserved at least a grateful hug.

The thought of throwing her arms around Gavin Buckley sent a quiver through Kate. Granted, he was a near stranger to her. But the incident at the cave had thrown them together in such a way that she couldn't help thinking of him as sort of a close, personal stranger. And that made her skin flush warmly, as though her arms were already around him.

The men had split up, Gavin ambling down the right side of the trail, and Mark taking the left. As he passed Zach Forrest, Gavin paused in midstride and studied the sullen boy as though he recognized him. Zach stared up at him, apparently puzzled. Then Gavin gave an almost imperceptible shake of his head, seeming to shake off a thought, and moved on past.

Mark hung back even longer, smiling at Lana, who frowned at him. He didn't appear to mind her frown. As Lana turned away from him, he seemed to catch sight of the butterfly tattoo on her shoulder.

He gave a soft whistle and murmured, "Well, hellooo, Butterfly."

Lana cut him a backward glance, scowling. After a moment, he hurried to catch up with Gavin.

The entire Camp Reliant group watched the men until they disappeared. Then Lana came up next to Kate and asked, "What was that all about?"

"Oh, it'd take too long to explain right now," Kate said, knowing full well that she could have squeezed it into one sentence. *Idiot that I am, I gave Gavin Buckley a shiner this morning when he tried to stop me from running out into the open and getting struck by lightning.* Changing the subject, she said, "Mark sure looked interested in you."

Lana made a face. "Ugh. He's too short."

Kate sighed again. "I guess we'd better get going, or we'll be late getting back to camp."

As the kids lined up and they resumed their climb, Kate kept glancing back down the trail toward the point where she had last seen Gavin and Mark. Even as she rounded the bend at the top of the trail and started downhill toward camp, she couldn't shake the strange feeling of connection that she had experienced under Gavin Buckley's mocking gaze.

Long after they had left the Camp Reliant bunch behind, Mark kept glancing back over his shoulder as if hoping against hope to catch one more look at them. Finally, he said, "Did you get a gander at that redhead with the butterfly tattoo?"

"Yeah." Gavin had thought the young woman looked about as sullen as the kid with the gold earring.

"Wasn't she something?" Mark asked, casting another hopeful glance over his shoulder. "Wonder what her name is."

Gavin made a noncommittal sound, thinking there was no accounting for taste.

Mark gave him a sardonic look. "What's tugging you, Gav?"

He shook his head. "Not a thing." Which was a long way from the truth.

"Sure." Mark smirked.

Gavin hated it when his friend smirked, which was precisely why Mark did it so often. "Eisly, you can be a royal pain. You know that?"

As they walked along in companionable silence, Gavin reflected on the boy with the gold earring. The kid had reminded him so much of himself at about that age that seeing him had triggered unwelcome flashbacks. Fortunately, they hadn't lasted long. Visions of Kate O'Riley had quickly nudged them back into the lockbox where Gavin had kept them for two decades.

"I guess I never realized I'm such a sucker for redheads," Mark said after a while.

"Give it a break, Mark. You've never even spoken to the girl, and you're already sounding obsessed."

"You think so?" Mark gave him a pensive look, followed by a crooked smile. "Well, I guess that's just what it feels like. Do you believe in love at first sight?"

"No, I do not."

"No? Well, you sure seemed interested in sweet Katie O'Riley."

"The woman came close to giving me a concussion, Mark. That's hard to ignore."

Mark nodded. "Yeah, and maybe it takes a Class A shiner to knock some sense into your head."

"What's that supposed to mean?"

"Oh, you'll figure it out one of these days," Mark said.

And there came the smirk again, as maddening as ever. Gavin made a growling sound, not having a clue what Mark was talking about.

A moment later, they approached the entrance to the cave system. Gavin found himself smiling as he recalled the look on Kate O'Riley's lovely face as she realized who he was. He would have given anything for a snap-shot of those remarkable amber eyes widening in shock.

He kept replaying that moment over and over again in his mind, until he caught Mark watching him.

"What?" Gavin asked.

"Don't look now, pal," Mark said, pausing in the cave entrance. "But maybe I'm not the only man on this mountain with an obsession."

Chapter Two

"**I** should've done this a long time ago." Cliff Peet dumped the last bucket of wet cement into the post hole and worked it in with a sharpshooter spade.

Kate peeled off her leather work gloves and dropped them into the empty wheelbarrow before stretching her tired back muscles. "Are you sure whoever owns this property won't mind your putting a gate on this cave entrance?" she asked.

"I'm sure." Cliff whipped a red bandana from the hip pocket of his overalls and mopped his bald head as they both sank down on a flat rock to rest. "I called and checked with the lawyer who represents the owner. He said the owner would be glad to pay for this work—said it beats being sued if one of our kids wandered into the cave and got lost or hurt."

"Lost?" Kate peered into the dark throat of the cave. "It's that big in there?"

He laughed. "Didn't you know? That's one of the entrances to a whole complex of caverns—miles of them, most likely. But they've never been mapped, so no one knows just how deep they go."

"I think someone's doing that now," she said.

When Cliff gave her a quizzical look, Kate told him about the two men she had met on the trail the previous afternoon. "They claimed they were surveying the cavern."

"Huh. Funny, the lawyer never mentioned that." He thought about it for a moment, and then frowned at her. "One of those fellows didn't happen to have a knot on his head, did he?"

Kate winced. She wished he hadn't reminded her of the little misunderstanding that had occurred after she had taken shelter from the storm. "Well, not exactly. It was more like a, uh, black eye."

"Seriously?" Cliff's frown deepened. "Did he recognize you when you ran into him again yesterday?"

She felt herself blush, recalling how Gavin Buckley had lifted his sunglasses to reveal those probing brown eyes. Well, eye. One, after all, had been nearly swollen shut. "I'd like to forget that whole incident," she said.

"When you hit him? Why? He tried to attack you, didn't he?"

"Well, you see, that was a mistake, Mr. Peet. My mistake, as it turns out." She knew she should have told him this yesterday, but she had been too embarrassed. "Gavin—that's his name, Gavin Buckley—was actually trying to stop me from running out into the lightning." She pointed to the lightning-blasted hickory tree on the steep slope next to the cave entrance.

Cliff scowled up at the old hickory for some time. Then he looked at Kate—and burst out laughing, slapping at both knees. Kate sat there feeling like ten kinds of fool, thinking she couldn't be more humiliated.

She was so wrong.

She heard a soft jangling sound behind her, and turned as Gavin Buckley stepped out of the dark cave into a shaft of bright sunlight. He wore the same yellow coveralls that he had the day before, and a hardhat with a carbide lantern identical to the one Cliff had found in the cave entrance the day before. A large coil of blue nylon rope was slung over one shoulder. He looked wet and dirty and tired—and as fit and strong as a mountain panther. He sported a crooked grin that made Kate wonder how long he'd been standing back there in the shadows, listening.

She quickly turned her back to him, suddenly wanting to crawl under the rock and hide. It was the same as when they'd met up on the trail the day before—that powerful desire to flee. And an equal desire to stay right where she was, close to Gavin.

She could feel her blush blossoming into a fiery shade of red that seemed to spread throughout her body. She didn't understand why she was reacting this way. If the handsome geologist was mocking her, she ought to be angry. But she wasn't. Not at all.

What she wanted more than anything else in the world at that moment was another chance. She wanted to go back twenty-four hours and meet Gavin Buckley for the first time all over again, without the black eye being an issue.

Cliff glanced over his shoulder, spotted Gavin, and rose. Reluctantly, so did Kate. Together, they watched Gavin descend the rocky incline in sure-footed, loose-jointed strides to join them.

Gavin thrust out his hand toward Cliff. "Gavin Buckley," he said.

"Figured as much." Cliff shook hands as he studied Gavin's shiner with interest.

Kate noticed that the swelling around the geologist's eye had gone down. But the bruise had changed from plum to Concord grape. It hurt her to look at it.

Finally, Cliff Peet introduced himself, adding. "I understand you and Kate, here, have met."

"Indeed we have." Still looking at Cliff, Gavin didn't try nearly hard enough to suppress a smile. The mirth at the corners of his mouth crept up his tanned, angular cheeks and danced in his warm brown eyes. Two eyes this time, with twice the emotional wattage of just one. "A couple of times."

Kate jammed her hands into the pockets of her shorts, still battling an urge to fade away out of sight. But that half-smile of Gavin's was beginning to get to her. She found that she couldn't help it—she had an almost overwhelming desire to smile herself. Only for some reason, that didn't seem right.

Still dangerously close to smiling outright, Gavin shifted his gaze to Kate. He seemed to look *into* her. She blinked once, and then their gazes locked. Deep inside her chest, a sensation swelled like a song without notes, thrumming there for some seconds before spreading rapidly outward to end in a distressingly pleasant tingle in her fingertips and toes. She had trouble taking her next breath.

A simple look had never affected Kate that way before. Then again, she was already certain that there was nothing simple about Gavin Buckley. After what seemed like an hour or two, he broke eye contact. Kate swallowed dryly, and then cleared her throat, vaguely aware that Cliff Peet had been watching the two of them with interest.

Gavin glanced around at the pair of newly-set metal posts, one on either side of the cave entrance. "What's going on here?"

"We're fixing to seal off the entrance," Cliff said, indicating the steel-barred gate that he and Toby Harris had dragged up from camp right after breakfast that morning. The gate looked sturdy enough to keep out a herd of elephants—or assorted curious youngsters bent on adventure.

Gavin arched an eyebrow. "This cave isn't on your property, you know."

"Mr. Peet got permission from the owner's lawyer," Kate put in, standing up for her boss.

Gavin looked surprised. "Rick Bonner?"

"He's the one," Cliff said.

"Is there something wrong with that?" Kate asked.

"Nope." Gavin stared off into space for several seconds before giving a shrug. "Need a hand?"

"Thanks, son." Cliff indicated the gate. "You might help me tote that thing up by the entrance. Once the cement's set around the posts, I'll bring help back up here to slip the gate into the brackets."

Gavin dropped his hardhat and coil of rope onto the ground and took up one end of the heavy gate. With a mighty grunt, Cliff hoisted the other end. Together the two men wrestled the gate up the stony incline and propped it against the lightning-blasted tree.

"No need to come back just to mount the gate, Mr. Peet," Gavin said. "I'll be up here every day this week. I can do the finishing up for you."

"It takes two to lift the dang thing."

"There are two of us. I work with a hydrologist."

"Oh? Doing what?"

"We're preparing a rough map of the cavern system

for my . . . for the owner. Nothing detailed. We're just checking to see if there's enough of interest in there to make a good tourist attraction."

Cliff's brows arched. "So what do you think?"

"So far, it's looking good."

"You don't say."

"Yep." Gavin raked a hand through his mahogany-colored hair, leaving it tousled across his wide forehead. He turned casually on one heel and looked down the slope at Kate. "Though I must say, it doesn't compare with the attractions out here."

His gaze again locked with hers, his expression curious this time, as if he hadn't quite made up his mind what to think of her. Kate's pulse quickened. The man didn't seem to hold his black eye against her as he had the day before—though even then he had half-joked about it. She thought that was incredibly generous of him.

Still, her lingering embarrassment over having inflicted the injury exactly counterbalanced her unexpected attraction to the lanky geologist. That made her feel as if she were precariously balanced on a teeter-totter—a teeter-totter that was, in turn, suspended above a deep crevasse.

"You live here in Greenbrier County?" Cliff asked, taking out the red bandana to swipe at his bald head once more.

Gavin shook his head without taking his gaze off Kate. "I teach at Penn State University. I'm just down here for the summer to help out my—" He aimed a thumb toward the cave entrance. "—the owner."

"You're a professor?" Kate asked. The man was full of surprises.

He nodded. "Of geology."

Silence stretched taut. When it seemed as though it might break from the tension, Cliff Peet stepped into the breech. "Now that I think about it, young fella, I know some Buckleys out around Covington. You any kin to them?"

"Sure am. I have an uncle up there named Morgan. He and Aunt Lil pretty much raised me and my sister."

Kate wanted to ask why Gavin's parents hadn't raised him—wanted to ask, but didn't, because she knew from experience with the kids whom she counseled at Camp Reliant that some things were difficult to talk about.

Cliff brightened. "Old Morgan Buckley's your uncle? Why, I've known him and Lil for, let's see, must be fifteen years now. They're good people. Morgan still raising horses?"

"He's mostly retired now."

"Good people," Cliff repeated, and seemed to warm to Gavin. "Listen, I have a chain and lock to go with this gate. Once it's installed, I'll be sure you get a key. Don't want to interfere with your mapping work."

Kate asked Gavin, "Who did you say you worked for?"

Gavin reached down and took his time picking up his hardhat and coil of rope. Kate had a distinct impression that he was stalling.

"I'm doing this work for an investor who'd rather remain anonymous until it's decided whether developing these caverns is worthwhile," he said.

She cocked a brow at what sounded like evasive words. "Why all the secrecy?"

He shrugged. "No secrecy, really. It's just too early to stir up a lot of public interest, when it all might come to nothing."

"But you said the caves are looking promising."

"Right."

"So . . . what's it like?" Kate peered into the darkness of the cave entrance. "I mean, are there rooms and things in there?"

"Big ones." Gavin leaned closer to murmur, "And wonders you can't imagine."

Something in his tone sent a thrill of excitement through her. Kate hugged herself. "Honest? You don't think it's . . . spooky?"

He grinned, his eyes dancing. "Spooky? Absolutely not. It's magic in there."

"Please, tell me about it."

Gavin studied her for a moment, looking her up and down from head to toe, as if carefully taking her measure. Then he shook his head slowly. "No, I can't describe it to you, Kate," he said, to her disappointment. "But if you'll let me, I'd take great pleasure in showing it to you."

Kate didn't know what to say. The prospect of actually venturing into the cave system had never entered her mind. But the shine that had come into Gavin Buckley's eyes began to melt her natural inclination to turn down his offer.

He seemed to sense her indecision, and added, "Kate, there are places down there that no human being has set eyes on since the beginning of time. It's like being the first person to step onto a new planet."

"I don't know . . ."

He grinned. "Come on. You'll love it. I guarantee."

She glanced toward the cave, still doubtful. "How do you know I will?"

"Trust me. And it'll change your life."

Anticipation welled up in Kate. *This is crazy,* she thought. She was letting herself be carried away by

Gavin Buckley's enthusiasm, and she hardly knew the man.

Then again, she argued with herself, thanks to the spectacular black eye that he now sported, she felt as if they'd known each other for ages. If Gavin could forgive her for the shiner, what possible harm could there be in letting him give her a tour of one of West Virginia's great natural wonders?

Kate turned to Cliff Peet, hoping for some guidance from her boss. He had moved off to one side and leaned against a tree, as if to give her and Gavin Buckley more space. She didn't quite know what to make of that. But when she looked at him, Cliff nodded encouragement.

"I always did want to know what was in there," Cliff said. "With my bum knee, I didn't figure I'd ever find out. But you're young and athletic, Katie. You go on in there with Gavin and have a look-see."

"We'll go first thing in the morning," Gavin said, as if the matter were settled.

"Wait just a doggone minute," Kate protested. "I didn't say I'd go."

"Why wouldn't you want to?" he said. "If these caverns are opened for tourists, you'll have to pay handsomely to see the sights that I can show you for free."

"Ah . . . now you're trying to appeal to my bank account."

He winked playfully. "Whatever works."

Kate rolled her eyes. But the fact was that she couldn't resist the lure of the caverns.

Well . . . no. That wasn't entirely true. She was excited about the prospect of seeing wonders that no one in history had ever seen before. But Gavin Buckley was what she really couldn't resist. There was something in the boyish wonder that kept leaping into his eyes when he talked about the caves.

That, and the warmth that glowed there when he looked at her.

The warmth wasn't all on his part. She felt it growing inside her as well. It made her tense and a little shaky. Too shaky. Kate wanted to draw back, catch her breath, and get her bearings. The caverns were uncharted terri-tory, but she sensed that Gavin Buckley represented an entire uncharted universe. She had a feeling that getting to know him better, if she chose to do that, would chal-lenge her courage.

"I'll do it," she heard herself say.

Before she could take back her words, Gavin reached out and clamped her upper arms with his big hands. "Right on!"

Cliff Peet began gathering up their tools. While Kate stood there flat-footed, he grabbed the handles of the wheelbarrow and started down the trail toward camp.

"Hang on there," Gavin said.

Cliff paused.

Gavin tossed his hardhat and rope into the wheelbar-row and took hold of the handles. "Let me tag along with you. I'll call the office from your place, and they can send someone to pick me up. Save me the hike back over the mountain."

"Suit yourself, son," Cliff said, happy to let the younger man take the lead. "Just follow this trail all the way down."

Kate glanced back at the cave entrance one last time, and then trotted after the two men, wondering what in the world she had gotten herself into.

* * *

The camp compound seemed unusually quiet, as if even the birds in the surrounding woods had forsaken the place. Kate stopped in the center of the clearing as Mr. Peet and Gavin trudged up the plank steps onto the porch of the main cabin. On the far side of the clearing, the pair of long dormitory cabins looked abandoned.

Then she heard the children's voices and caught a whiff of fried chicken.

She glanced at her watch. Helping Mr. Peet set the gate posts hadn't taken as long as she had imagined. The kids were still having lunch at the covered picnic tables behind the main cabin. The afternoon balance-beam session wasn't scheduled to begin for another forty minutes.

Kate climbed the steps and stood in the cool shade beneath the deep overhang of the porch. The sun was shining for a change, after so many days of rain. She closed her eyes and filled her lungs with the sweet smell of damp woods, aware of how much she love the mountains and her job at Camp Reliant. She just wished she didn't sometimes feel so overpowered by both.

From inside the cabin, she could hear Gavin on the phone, giving someone instructions on how to reach Camp Reliant. She smiled, looking forward to their little adventure tomorrow. The thought of spending time with Gavin filled her with jittery anticipation.

Her reverie was cut short by the sound of a child's angry squeal. Kate murmured, "What now?" and dropped down off the porch.

She was halfway around the cabin heading for the picnic tables when a youngster came barreling toward her. Kate dashed to her left and snagged Zach Forrest by the belt, spinning him to a halt.

"Whoa, there," she siad. "What's going on?"

Zach struggled for a few seconds, then gave up and

went still, sulking. She could feel the heat of his anger pouring off him, and wondered what had caused it this time.

Kate was beginning to lose faith that she would ever be able to get through to the boy.

She let go of his belt. Zach didn't try to run off, but he refused to look her in the face. Instead he stared defiantly off to one side, his raven hair sweated onto his forehead, his earring glinting in the noonday sun. He was such a good-looking boy, with the intense, bright eyes of a poet or a scientist. Beneath his rebellious façade, his obvious misery once again made Kate doubt her skills as a counselor.

"What's the problem?" she asked, wanting to add *this time.*

"Stupid rules."

"Which ones?" She smiled, trying to keep judgment out of her voice. "Or do you have a bone to pick with rules in general?"

"Counselor Lana just chewed me out because I took a walk. A stinking walk! Isn't that what we're supposed to do here? Get plenty of fresh air and exercise?"

"Uh-huh." Kate bit her lip. Lana knew better than to "chew out" any of the kids, under any circumstances. All serious infractions were supposed to be taken to Lana's father to handle. Cliff Peet had a talent for dealing with this sort of thing, firmly, but in a way that made everyone feel they had learned something positive.

She smoothed the shock of hair off Zach's forehead. He jerked his head away from her, but didn't protest when she rested a hand on his narrow shoulder. "How long were you gone on this walk, Zach?"

He shrugged. "Not long."

"Ten minutes?"

He nodded.

"An hour?"

Zach hesitated, and then nodded again.

He had a temper, and he didn't like rules, but the boy never lied. Kate had learned that about him early on. The challenge, she knew, was in asking the right questions.

"Zach, you know you aren't supposed to leave camp without supervision. This isn't a park out here. You could get lost."

He hunched his shoulders and clammed up. Kate felt as if she could reach out and touch the invisible wall that the boy had thrown up around himself. But she didn't know how to break through the barrier, much less climb over it. She told herself that she should know how to deal with this child. But with every passing day, he had made her feel less adequate as a counselor.

If she didn't break through to him soon, Kate thought, she was going to require some counseling herself.

"So who let out that scream a minute ago?" she asked.

"Who do you think?" he said. "Annie Rich."

"Ah. And what was her problem?"

Zach gave a snort of derision. "A cricket went down her shirt."

"Interesting. How do you suppose that happened?"

Zach looked her in the eye then. "She laughed at me. I was standing there while Counselor Lana was laying down the law, and Annie Rich laughed at me. And because she laughed, so did the others."

Kate silently groaned. Her heart told her that the boy needed a hug at that moment a lot more than he needed to be called on the carpet one more time. But she was afraid he might see a hug as a reward for putting a cricket down Annie Rich's shirt—if he let Kate put her arms around him at all. Zach was a loner, and he did all he could to keep himself that way.

"Zach, we all want to help you," she said. "But *you* have to want your stay here at Camp Reliant to work."

He had clammed up again.

Confronted by his stubbornness, Kate had to admit that she had met her match, at least for the moment. But she wasn't about to give up on the boy. Because if she gave up on Zach Forrest, she figured she might as well give up on herself as a counselor. And for a long time now, being a counselor—helping kids just like Zach—had been the biggest dream in her life.

"Zach," she said gently, "you know we'll have to tell Mr. Peet that you left camp without supervision."

The hard set of his jaw said that he didn't care. But the tears in his eyes said that pretending that he didn't care came at a price.

Kate touched his shoulder. "You go back and finish eating with the other kids. We can deal with this after lunch."

"I don't want to eat lunch. I want to go home."

"You will, hon. In less than a week. Meanwhile, I know you'll want your mom to be proud—"

"Nobody cares what I want!" Zach shouted, and bolted past her.

Kate called out to the boy, but he ignored her. Zach had almost reached the front of the cabin when Gavin Buckley strode around the corner and the two collided head-on. Zach ricocheted off the geologist, and would have fallen flat if Gavin hadn't caught him.

"What the devil . . . ?" Gavin held onto Zach by one arm and looked at Kate. "I thought I heard an argument."

"It was one-sided," Kate said wearily. "Thanks, Gavin. But let him go."

Gavin looked at her as if she had asked him to go jump off the roof. "I don't think so," he said. He turned Zach around to face her. "From what I heard a few seconds ago, I'd say this young gentleman owes you an apology."

"Gavin, please. You don't understand. That isn't how we operate here at Camp Reliant."

He looked confused, and not particularly happy about it. "You mean you let kids get away with talking to you that way?" He frowned down at Zach, who stared off into the distance as if his behavior weren't the sole focal point of two adults.

"Gavin, please," Kate repeated evenly, though her stomach was in a knot. She was worried sick over Zach—and now Gavin had thrown an altogether different wrench into the works by unwittingly putting her very authority into question right there in front of the boy. "I know you mean well, but this isn't a good time to get into this." She stretched a smile that made Gavin frown. "Let Zach go. I'll explain—"

"No need to explain anything." Gavin's tone was light, but she could tell he disapproved. "You know what you're doing."

I hope so, Kate thought. *Oh, I sincerely hope so.*

Gavin whipped his hand away from Zach as if he were releasing a red-hot poker.

Zach shot Kate a look that wasn't in the least grateful for her help in securing his freedom, then whirled away and streaked around the corner of the cabin out of sight. She couldn't help noticing, and not for the first time, that Zach Forrest had the ability to outrun any kid in Camp Reliant.

If he wanted to.

Which he never had.

Gavin stood with his fists on his lean hips, scowling after Zach. As she watched him, Kate realized she was breathing hard, as if it were her and not Zach who had just sprinted away.

A moment later, she heard a screen door slap shut. She was pretty sure that was the door to the boys' dormitory.

"Well," Gavin said after a long silence. "I guess I stuck my nose someplace it didn't belong."

"Oh, Gavin, I do appreciate your trying to help. But forcing—demanding—an apology from Zach isn't how it works here. Camp Reliant is all about learning to make choices. A lot of these kids have learned to make *wrong* choices, or no choices at all. They have to be shown that there is power in making right choices. But the power in those choices is in their hands, not ours. If we try to force these kids to make our choices instead of their own, they'll see that the power is totally in *our* hands. Then what will they have learned?"

Gavin reached up and rubbed the back of his neck as he eyed Kate. For some reason, it was important to her that he understand the philosophy behind Camp Reliant, and that he believe in the program as much as she did. But his expression seemed to be at war with itself, changing rapidly back and forth between irritation and puzzlement. At last, it settled on something akin to grudging acceptance.

"All right, Kate. You're the boss."

"Well, no. As a matter of fact, Cliff Peet is the boss." She tried a smile again. "I'm just a first-year counselor trying to keep my head above water. I never knew kids could be so . . ."

"Knot-headed?"

Kate chuckled. "I was going to say 'strong-willed.' At Zach's age, I was such a mouse."

Gavin studied her again, hard, as he had back at the cave entrance—as if he were taking her measure. She felt her self-doubt over Zach being replaced by another kind of uncertainty. Gavin Buckley did that to her, making her feel as if the ground under her feet were shifting. Kate found the sensation at the same time disturbing and thrilling.

"No, Kate," he said quietly. "You're dead-wrong about that. You can't have ever been a mouse. Not for real. But there's this other thing too. You're wrong about that boy." He nodded back toward where they had last seen Zach rounding the corner of the cabin, and then pointed a finger straight at her. "Dead wrong."

With that, Gavin turned and walked away.

Kate didn't move. For a moment, she *couldn't* move. Then her head cleared, and she knew she couldn't just leave their conversation hanging in midair like that.

She caught up with Gavin on the front porch of the main cabin. He sat on the top step, watching the road that led up to the camp from the highway. When he saw her coming, he gave her a rueful smile.

"Sorry about my attitude back there, Kate," he said. "I've been told I'm a man of stubborn convictions."

She sat down next to him and wrapped her arms around her knees. "Gavin, I know our methods here at Camp Reliant are sometimes difficult for outsiders to grasp. Especially when you see a child like Zach going through a rough spell." *'Rough spell,'* Kate thought, was a major understatement. "But the program really does help most of our kids."

He looked at her. "Not all of them?"

She shook her head. "There's no such thing as one

size fits all. But Camp Reliant works for most of them. It worked for me."

Gavin tilted his head and studied her with renewed interest. "You went through the program?"

"When I was twelve. That's why I'm here now. I want to give back some of what I got."

A gust of wind tossed his hair across his forehead. Gavin didn't seem to notice, so intently was he eyeing Kate. She felt her skin warm, and blamed it on the bright sunlight.

After a moment, Gavin shifted his gaze back toward the road, watching for his ride back to town.

"I don't know, Kate," he said. "I still have trouble standing by and letting a kid get away with rude behavior. I was a second-hand kid, raised by parents who weren't my own. Like your boss said, my aunt and uncle are good people. I wouldn't have dreamed of talking back to them."

Kate rested her chin on her knees, wondering again what had happened to his real parents, but not asking. "Kids respond to their environment in different ways, Gavin. Some are more resilient than others. It isn't fair to expect one to be as strong as the next. We just need to be around for those who need us, to help them find their strengths."

He grinned without looking at her. "You think I need an attitude adjustment."

"A bit."

"Well, you'd get my sister's vote. She'd love you if you belted me." He reached up and fingered his bruised eye. "Again."

"You have a sister?"

"A twin."

"Neat."

Gavin barked a laugh. "You don't know Mickie."

Kate heard a truck engine grinding up the long drive-way, and felt a pang of disappointment. She'd been enjoying sitting there on the porch step talking with Gavin Buckley. The more she was around the geologist, the less he rattled her. She was beginning to find him . . . interesting. Perhaps even something more than that.

A bright yellow Hummer came into view at the head of the driveway. Kate recognized Mark Eisly at the wheel, and waved to him. Gavin shoved himself to his feet and gathered up his caving gear as the vehicle rolled to a stop at the edge of the clearing.

"Well, I'd better get on back to town." Gavin paused, as if reluctant to leave. "I'll see you at the cave tomorrow morning? Nine o'clock sharp?"

"Sounds good to me." Kate felt a flutter of excitement over getting a look at the cavern, not to mention being alone with Gavin.

He walked backwards a couple of paces toward the waiting Hummer, smiling at Kate, then turned and strode away.

Chapter Three

The next morning while the kids were at breakfast under Lana Peet's supervision, Kate met with Cliff Peet and Toby Harris in the main cabin. Toby slouched in an old Eames chair in Peet's upstairs office. The tall, muscular senior counselor had the broad shoulders of a football linebacker. His sheer size might have made him intimidating to the kids were it not for his gentle voice and ready smile.

"The humidity is so heavy you could stir it with a stick," he said.

"There's gonna be more rain," Peet agreed, pacing the room and rubbing his shoulder. "I can feel it in my joints."

"Maybe it'll hold off until nightfall and not interfere with today's program," Kate said, knowing very well that nobody disputed Cliff Peet's "weather shoulder." His arthritic joints acted up with every shift in the barometer.

"We'll work it out, rain or shine," said Toby. "The kids have made excellent progress."

"With the exception of the Forrest boy." Peet stopped pacing and gave the two counselors a penetrating scowl. "I heard that Lana read Zach Forrest the Riot Act yesterday noon."

Kate looked uneasily at Toby, who shrugged.

"I spent the lunch hour working on the sand pit out at the obstacle course," Toby said. "Didn't see a thing."

"How about you, Kate?" Peet asked.

"Well, I didn't see it either." Kate hated being put on the spot where Mr. Peet's daughter was concerned. And yet, it wasn't as if she were telling him anything he apparently didn't already know. "Zach did mention that Lana had chewed him out at lunch."

Peet winced. "In front of the other kids?"

"It seems so."

He turned his back on them and stared out the window. Kate could tell he was embarrassed and disappointed that his daughter had violated his rule against upbraiding any child in front of his or her peers. If the redness rising up the back of his neck was any indication, Peet also was angry.

"Mr. Peet, Lana will grow into the job," Kate said, though she harbored some serious doubts on that account.

"I hope you're right," he said. "But I'm beginning to wonder. She's become so . . ."

So brittle, thought Kate, realizing for the first time that Lana Peet and Zach Forrest had a lot in common.

"Look," she said, "maybe I shouldn't be traipsing off on a tour of the cave system this morning."

"Nonsense, Kate." Peet checked his watch as he turned from the window. "Toby and I'll have the kids busy polishing their tracking skills until mid-afternoon. Besides, you've been carrying more than your share of the load lately." His look said that he understood how she had been taking up Lana's slack all summer. "You need a change of pace. Now scoot."

He pointed to the door.

She glanced at Toby, who smiled and waggled his fingers at her. She got up, and hesitated at the door only briefly before hurrying out. She didn't want to keep Gavin waiting.

Kate got a later start than intended. To keep from being late, she had to make the hike up the steep mountain trail almost at a trot. By the time she reached the cave, she was hot, sweaty, and out of breath.

Gavin was waiting. When she saw him seated at the cave entrance, her heart beat even faster.

She noticed right away that Gavin and Mark Eisly had installed the gate on its posts. They'd already been busy that morning.

When Gavin spotted Kate huffing toward him up the trail, he got to his feet. He was wearing his usual yellow coveralls, which seemed to be his all-purpose spelunking uniform. At his feet was a well-worn duffel bag.

"Forgive me for being late," she said, scrambling up the slope to join him at the entrance. She had brought a heavy chain and padlock with her. She dumped them on the ground next to the gate.

Gavin's smile made the corners of his eyes crinkle. "What's ten minutes among friends?" He handed her a gray sweatshirt bearing a Penn State logo, then a hardhat with a carbide lamp strapped to it. "Here, I brought you something warm to wear."

Kate frowned at the sweatshirt, which looked big enough to have been one of his. "Gavin, it's the middle of summer. Or haven't you noticed?"

He chuckled. "It's never summer inside a mountain, Kate. I forgot to warn you about that yesterday. You'd better put it on."

She did as she was told, though without a great deal of enthusiasm. The sweatshirt swallowed her. But she pushed the sleeves up to her elbows and donned the hardhat.

"All set?" Gavin asked, and led the way into the cave without waiting for her response.

"Where is Mark?" she asked, following close behind.

"Farther up the mountain, scouting for other cave entrances."

"There are more?"

"Could be."

Gavin halted suddenly, and Kate almost bumped into him. She asked, "What's wrong?"

"Well, nothing's *wrong*. At least I hope not." He bent and picked up something off the cave floor. "But it looks like we got that gate up a shade too late."

He showed her a whistle on a woven leather lanyard, like all the kids wore. Kate held the whistle toward the wan light penetrating from the entrance, and could just make out the initials ZF scratched into the metal.

"It's Zach's." Her heart sank at the realization that the boy apparently had been exploring inside the cave all alone.

Gavin unclipped a metal flashlight from his belt and shone the narrow beam deeper into the cave.

Still shaken by Zach's trespass, Kate slipped the whistle and lanyard into her pocket. "Don't worry, Gavin, he isn't here. I saw him back at Camp Reliant just before I left."

"That's a relief. I'll be sure to lock the gate when we

leave." Gavin smiled at Kate. "Now, my lady, we'd better get started."

He removed his hardhat, lit its carbide lantern, and then did the same for Kate's. Shouldering the duffel bag, he took Kate's hand and led her on into the cave.

Within minutes, they had passed through the twilight-zone of indirect light near the entrance, and entered the realm of visual midnight. At first, Kate found the darkness unnerving. But Gavin's hand was reassuring, and she gradually adjusted to using her lantern to illuminate the surrounding stone.

"This is sedimentary rock," Gavin said some time later, releasing her to run his hand over the cave wall. His voice had grown softer the farther they went along, until he was almost whispering. "It took a million years—maybe ten million years—of water trickling through cracks and crevices to eat away the limestone and create these caves."

"Wow," she whispered, automatically following his lead.

"Yeah. The wet areas deeper inside the mountain are still active, still being slowly etched out."

Kate touched the wall with her fingertips, trying to wrap her mind around such an ancient process. "How deep do you suppose this cave system goes?"

"Hard to say. Mark and I have been a mile deep. For all we know, that might be just the beginning."

She halted and stared at him. "You're kidding."

"I'm serious as rain. But the passages don't run in a straight line. They run off in all directions, sometimes cutting back on themselves or opening into cavernous rooms. Like a maze with no pattern."

All the more reason to keep a locked gate on the entrance, Kate thought. Back in the direction from which

Sandra Dark

they had come, not so much as a glimmer of light penetrated the cave. The very idea of a child getting lost in the ink-black warren of passages made her shudder.

Gavin noticed, and took her hand again. "Hey, relax. You're going to love this."

The warmth of his touch and the quiet eagerness in his voice boosted Kate's confidence. When he squeezed her hand, a sudden thrill raced up her arm. She smiled, and squeezed back.

They moved on, alternately walking and crawling along twisting corridors of limestone. The farther they went, the more grateful Kate was that Gavin had loaned her the sweatshirt. In the heart of a mountain, she guessed the temperature to be down in the fifties. But the exercise, along with Gavin's occasional touch as he helped her negotiate tight places or steep climbs, kept her from feeling chilled.

After a while, time and distance lost all shape. Kate was conscious only of the surrounding stone, the chilly air, and Gavin Buckley's reassuring presence.

Later still, she grew edgy in the eternal night that was broken only by the shifting wash of their lanterns. She had no idea where they were going or how long Gavin intended their subterranean adventure to last. Not knowing that made their exploration seem all the more aimless and disorienting.

As he took her hand to help her over a rockfall, she asked, "How much farther?"

He laughed. The sound reverberated off the limestone walls, and she realized at last why they had been whispering. "Patience, Kate. I think you'll find that where we're going is well worth the walk."

"What walk?" she asked wryly. The ceiling of the passage had lowered, and they had been crawling on their hands and knees for some distance.

"Okay, I can take a hint." Gavin stopped to check his compass and give them both a rest.

The cave was growing damp. As they sat on their heels, knee to knee, Gavin dug into his duffel bag and produced a granola bar. He split it with her, carefully tucking the empty wrapper back into the bag.

"Gavin, I'm so turned around, I don't even know which way is up."

He grinned and pointed at the ceiling a foot above their heads. "I'm pretty sure that's up."

She swatted him playfully on the knee, thinking he had a great smile.

During their progress through the cave system, she had discovered that Gavin Buckley was given to long silences. She found that she liked that about him too.

Kate wolfed down the meager snack. She hadn't thought to bring food of her own, and now that omission loomed large. "I'm starved out of my mind," she admitted.

"And your legs are killing you. And your back aches. And your shoes are full of rocks."

"How did you know?"

"Because I'm in the same shape. I also need to change the carbide in our lanterns. Three hours is about their limit."

"Three hours?" She cringed at the sound of her own voice reverberating off limestone.

"Yup. But hang in there, and I'll take care of your appetite in about two shakes."

Gavin turned and crawled off up the passage. Kate followed at a safe distance, aware that the carbide lantern on her hardhat was an open flame.

Two sharp right-angle turns, and they started up a steep incline. As Gavin helped her traverse the slippery clay surface, Kate spotted a horizontal crevice just ahead. He reached it first, and braced one foot against a rock.

"Ladies first," he said, standing to one side of the opening.

Kate gave him a startled look. He waited. Finally she relented and eased her upper body into the cocoon of darkness, not in the least excited about leading the way into the unknown. As she wriggled along the banana-shaped passage, she wished Gavin had gone first. And yet she had to admit that Gavin had made her feel like a veteran caver by insisting that she go first.

She could hear him worming his way along after her, whisper-whistling through his teeth, shoving his duffel bag ahead of him.

Suddenly she cried, "I'm through!" and spilled head-first out the other end.

"Watch your step," he called. "Don't fall into the moonmilk."

Moonmilk? Certain that she had misunderstood, Kate scrambled to her feet. She turned back to the crevice just in time to catch the duffel bag. Gavin followed seconds later.

"You look like you're taking off a stone girdle," she said when his chest was clear.

"Maybe that's why women are usually better at this."

Kate watched him extrude from the rock like a moth working itself free of its cocoon. "What if you get stuck?"

"You'd go for help."

"With you blocking the exit?"

"This isn't the only way out, just the shortest. You could find another."

"Fat chance. I'd never find my way out of here."

"Sure you would. It's just a matter of wandering around until you find the right passage, assuming of course that you have a light. No light, and all bets are off." He slid free of the crevice and staggered to his feet.

Gavin unzipped his duffel bag and dug out a smaller bag, which he handed to Kate. "Here. Lunch."

"Lunch? Oh, you wonderful man."

He sat her down on a slab of limestone and left her to investigate the contents of the bag while he shouldered the duffel and wandered off on his own. For several minutes, Kate was engrossed in sorting through sandwiches, trail mixes, and foil packets of dried fruits. As famished as she was, the food looked fit for a king.

When she finally looked up from the bounty, she gasped.

The tight crawl through the crevice a moment earlier had delivered them into a huge limestone chamber. While she foraged in the lunch bag, Gavin had placed half a dozen collapsible-glass lamps containing small slow-burning candles around the spacious cavern. The soft candlelight illuminated a stunning array of towering calcite columns, squat stalagmites, and gracefully tapered stalactites. The formations dripped with water, glistening like jewels in the wavering light.

Gaping, Kate craned her neck in amazement. This, she realized, must be the cavern-in-the-making that Gavin had mentioned hours ago.

Several pools enclosed by high rims were clustered near the center of the chamber. Kneeling beside the largest one, Gavin motioned for Kate to join him. Clutching the lunch bag, she crept over to his side.

"Moonmilk." He indicated the milky water filling the pool. "It's mostly calcite suspended in water. But in some warm limestone caves, the solution contains bacteria that have been studied as sources of antibiotics."

"I had no idea . . ." Kate trailed her fingers through the chilly liquid.

"And look at this." Gavin reached in and scooped out several round objects. "Cave pearls. They're pretty rare in caves that have been explored, because they're so easy to carry off."

"Does that mean this cave hasn't had many visitors?"

"Mark and I have come across no signs of humans down here in the wet zone."

"You mean . . . we three are the *only* human beings who've ever seen all this?" Kate swept an arm wide, taking in the spectacular formations.

He grinned. "Thrilling, isn't it?"

"I feel so . . .." Kate had to search for the right word. ". . . honored."

Her choice seemed to surprise Gavin. He studied her for a long moment, then reached out and lightly brushed the back of a forefinger across her cheek.

Kate gasped, and then smiled.

His touch warmed her despite the chill of the cavern. She sat very still, wondering if Gavin were going to kiss her because the look in his eyes said he definitely wanted to. And—oh, yes—she found that she wanted him to.

She was just beginning to wonder what that would be like, when he suddenly cleared his throat and turned away to restore the cave pearls to their rightful place in the pool.

A little relieved, a little disappointed, and a whole lot embarrassed that she must have read too much into his gaze, Kate opened the lunch bag and pulled out a sandwich. She worried that if Gavin had seen the desire in her own eyes, he must think she was—

She shoved that thought right out of her mind.

Gavin settled down by the rimstone pool. She handed him a sandwich and took a quick look around. Deciding that he had the best seat in the house, she sat down beside him and stretched out her legs alongside his.

Kate unwrapped her sandwich and lifted its lid to check the contents. "Oh, wow. Peanut butter and grape jelly. You're such a gourmet."

He grinned again. "Takes you back to when you were a kid, doesn't it?"

"Or to my last all-day hike, which was last Thursday."

He watched her as he ate. "You really love those kids you work with, don't you?"

"Love them?" Kate gave that some thought. "Yeah, you're right. I guess I see so much of myself in them."

Something flickered in his eyes. For just an instant, she thought Gavin identified on some deep level with what she had just said. But then it was gone, and he was looking at her with uncomplicated interest as he worked on his sandwich.

"As an only child, I was such a shy little mouse of a kid," she went on. "Without Cliff Peet and Camp Reliant, I never would have developed the self-confidence to try to do the things I really want to accomplish in life."

"Such as?"

"Such as making a difference in other people's lives. Especially kids. Build up a child's self-esteem, and that child has the power to dream. And a dream . . . well, a dream can take you almost anywhere."

"If you work at it."

"Oh, yes." Kate smiled, momentarily enthralled by the candlelight dancing in his eyes. She had to glance away to scrabble her thoughts back together. "Making a dream come true is always hard work, Gavin. I went to college

Sandra Dark

first, then came back and applied for a job at Camp Reliant."

They ate in silence for a few minutes. Kate had no idea that peanut butter and jelly could taste so good. But now that they weren't moving around, the damp chill of the cavern was sinking in. She shivered.

"Cold?" Gavin reached out and pulled her close against him. She resisted for just a second before settling in under his enveloping arm. All around them, light from the candles leaped and cavorted over the fanciful calcite formations.

Kate wondered if the magical place that Gavin Buckley had brought her to was responsible for how at ease she felt with him. No doubt about it, she was attracted to the geologist—and sitting there with his arm around her in the cathedral-like silence was more romantic than she ever would have thought possible. But this felt deeper than that.

This felt like something as real and substantial as the limestone cavern itself.

That thought suddenly seemed overpowering. Maybe they were too close, she decided, and reluctantly moved far enough away so that she could see Gavin's face.

"What about you?" Kate asked, forcing conversation into the silence. "What's your family like?" She could have bitten her tongue as soon as the words were out of her mouth. She had forgotten that he and his sister were raised by an aunt and uncle—a potentially touchy subject.

He stared into the distance for a moment before responding. "My mother . . . well, she and Dad had a parting of the ways. It wasn't pretty." He made "wasn't pretty" sound like a gross understatement.

"How old were you?"

"My sister and I were nine."

"Gavin, I'm sorry about your folks. Divorce is rough on a child." She had seen the results of that trauma in many of the youngsters at Camp Reliant that summer. "It must be a painful thing to look back on as an adult."

He shrugged. "We did all right. Aunt Lil and Uncle Morgan stepped in, and they couldn't have been better to Mickie and me. After a while . . . quite a while . . . it got to feeling like a regular family again. The four of us hung together and supported one another."

"You respected one another."

Gavin nodded, and Kate began to understand why he had seemed so affronted by Zach Forrest's behavior the day before.

"Do you see your parents much?"

"My real ones?" He shook he head. "Mother moved to the West Coast after the divorce. Dad's down in Houston."

And they had left their children to be raised by relatives. "You must have felt abandoned," Kate said. "To be left behind with your aunt and uncle."

Gavin opened a package of trail mix, responding to her statement with a silence that spoke for itself.

"Well," she said, thinking that abandonment by one's parents was bound to leave an indelible impression, "fortunately all marriages don't end in disaster."

He gave her a droll look that didn't seem to fit the tone of the subject. "Maybe not. But it seems like a pretty risky roll of the dice."

Gavin's risk-assessment of marriage startled Kate, especially coming from a man who found such pleasure in exploring uncharted caverns. Her own parents enjoyed a solid marriage, and she had always considered that contract to be a vital element of any couple's relationship. So much so that she couldn't imagine marriage not being a natural and inevitable progression of love. Gavin's serious misgivings about that issue left her feeling sorry for him.

Wishing now that she hadn't broached the subject of his family, she slid from the warmth of his arm and shifted the lunch bag onto her lap. Gavin seemed perplexed by her sudden move, but before he could say anything, she changed the subject.

"Do you want another of these sandwiches?" she asked, fishing through the depleted contents of the bag.

"Nope. One more and I won't be able to squeeze back through there." He pointed toward the narrow crevice through which they had wriggled. "I have a serious weight problem," he said with a smile.

"Oh, yeah?" Kate had been leaning against his hard body, and knew he was as lean as a greyhound. "Where?"

Gavin chuckled. "Kate, I didn't say I was overweight, but there was a time when I was known to eat one too many super-sized cheeseburger meals."

She had seen children of divorced parents take out their grief on food, and wondered if that had been his problem. Still, "I can't imagine you ever being . . ."

"Chubby?" he offered. "My friends called me Tank."

"Some friends."

His grin turned to a grimace. "My scout master took a bunch of us caving one weekend. It was my first time, and it turned out to be the most mortifying experience of my life, even to this day."

She knew she shouldn't keep probing into the man's

life, but she couldn't seem to help herself. "I'm all ears."

"And nose." He reached out and tweaked the tip of Kate's nose. "Anyway, I got stuck in a tight spot, and having the others help me out was a little more than embarrassing. I swore then and there that I'd never let something like that happen again."

"But you didn't let that experience keep you from falling in love with . . ." she swept her gaze over the candlelit cavern, ". . . all this."

"Caving was a challenge in the beginning, nothing more and nothing less. But once you've discovered something like this—been where no other living being has ever set foot . . ." He sighed. "Well, it's sort of like being in outer space without ever having left Earth. There's an inner space down here that fills you up."

They sat quietly for a while, soaking in the enveloping silence. It seemed to work itself into Kate's pores like a palpable element.

Eventually, Kate became aware that Gavin was watching her. When she glanced at him, he averted his gaze. He was smiling slightly as if to himself.

A moment later, he said, "Maybe we could split one of those sandwiches."

"No way." She hugged the bag. "What's happening to your self-control?"

He looked at her again, his gaze entwining with hers. Her mouth went dry, and her pulse quickened to that rising gallop that was becoming so familiar when she was around Gavin. Kate felt the heat of a blush rising up her neck, and was grateful for the dim light.

"Right now, Kate, my self-control is in about the same shape as yours," he said softly. "Stumbling all over itself."

The softness of his voice, the gentle glow of his eyes, took her breath away. The light dimmed. A distant corner of her mind registered that one of the candle lanterns had flickered out.

He definitely wants to kiss me, Kate thought. Though she suddenly wanted to be kissed, she also had a wild urge to run away. And stay right there in the candlelit cavern with Gavin Buckley. Rattled by the unexpected turn their conversation had taken and by the way he was looking at her—as if he had just discovered a rare and amazing gem—she scrambled to her feet.

Gavin started to rise. Kate tried to step out of his way, and her feet slipped out from under her on the wet limestone. He made a grab for her. She fell clumsily against him, and they held their balance just long enough to share a startled laugh. For mere seconds, his lips were close to Kate's, his breath warm on her face.

She didn't even realize they were falling until they hit the frigid moonmilk.

Morning had long since turned to afternoon by the time Kate and Gavin finally emerged from the cave system. As they stepped from the mouth of the cave, a loud boom of thunder greeted them.

Gavin glanced up at a threatening sky. So did Kate. Still soaking wet from the tumble into the rimstone pool, she looked too exhausted to be disheartened by yet another storm. He figured that all she cared about right then was getting back to Camp Reliant and into dry clothes.

The trip down into the cavern hadn't turned out as Gavin had hoped. It had been important to him that Kate came away from it enchanted by the wonders that existed inside the mountain. For a while there, he thought he was succeeding. She really had appeared to be fascinated by the chamber and its moonmilk pools.

But then all that seemed to come unraveled while they sat around talking while eating lunch. Maybe he hadn't been paying enough attention, but he wasn't sure exactly what had caused Kate to draw away from him. He just knew that she had, suddenly, as if a curtain had fallen between them.

Though she had seemed friendly and talkative enough as they made their way back out of the system, Gavin could sense that curtain between them still. And it bothered him. It bothered him a whole lot. Because right about the time that invisible barrier fell between them, he had begun to get it through his thick skull that Mark Eisly just might have a point. Gavin hated to admit that Mark was right about such matters, but there it was, staring him smack in the face—he was interested in Kate O'Riley.

Interested, my eye, he thought. *You're fascinated, old buddy. How do you like them apples?*

As a matter of fact, he liked it just fine. Being hooked on Katie O'Riley felt good . . . even exhilarating.

But there was that inexplicable curtain. That worried him.

Gavin secured the gate with the chain and padlock that Kate had brought up from camp. When he was confident that no kids from Camp Reliant would be able to get through the barrier, he gathered up his gear. Then he took Kate's hand and they hurried down the trail.

Chapter Four

By ten o'clock that night, every muscle in Kate's body begged her to go straight to bed. But as she stepped out of the shower smelling of honeysuckle shampoo, she knew she wouldn't be hitting the sack right away. She had one more thing to do first.

After blowing her hair dry, she slipped into a light-weight cotton warm-up suit and sneakers. Then she left her room and crept down the hallway to the front door, being as quiet as possible in case Toby and the Peets were already asleep.

Moonlight cast inky shadows across the clearing. Kate paused on the porch to breathe in the pine-scented night air. From somewhere off in the woods came the sharp twitter of a small bird, perhaps disturbed on its perch by a hunting owl.

Across the clearing, dim yellow light burned on the porches of the two dormitory cabins. Otherwise, nothing stirred. As usual, the kids had been run ragged all day, and then fed hardy suppers. By this time of the night, most of them were sound asleep.

Most, but not all.

And that was what had drawn Kate out on this night, as it had nearly every night of the past several weeks.

She stepped down off the porch of the main cabin and started across the clearing, moving in and out of shadows that shifted and danced in the gusty night breeze. Fallen pine needles silenced the sound of her footsteps, but she could hear the whisper of the breeze through the surrounding treetops.

How strange, she thought, that she had whiled away the better part of the day in darkness and silence more complete than any night. And yet, when she thought back on the fleeting hours that she had spent exploring the nearby cavern system with Gavin Buckley. her mind conjured not darkness, but images of stunning beauty.

Lantern light washing over ancient limestone. Candlelight flickering over fantastical columns and spires of calcite. Cave pearls and moonmilk, and the complicated man who had led her on that memorable journey of discovery.

Kate realized that she had stopped in the middle of the clearing and was staring dreamily up at the stars. With a sigh, she moved on to the boys' dormitory.

She tiptoed up the steps. The screen door whined faintly on its hinges as she opened it and slipped inside. Two pale nightlights glowed along the wall to her right, emitting just enough light so that she could make out the shapes on the cots.

Kate made her way down the wide center aisle, detouring once to tuck a sheet over a sleeping Tommy Reyes. At the end of the aisle, she stopped at the foot of Zach Forrest's cot.

The boy lay on his side in a tangle of sheets, curled up in a tight ball, both fists clinched in front of his face.

Each night, Zach looked as if he were going to war with his dreams. Each night, Kate's heart went out to him.

She moved to the side of the cot and knelt, as silent as a shadow. With her face less than a foot from Zach's, she could hear the faint, fitful whisper of a nightmare escaping his lips. As she had on so many other nights, Kate strained to hear the words, but all she could make out was his distress.

Kate reached out and placed a hand ever so gently on the side of Zach's sweating head. He tensed even more, but didn't awaken. She stroked his hair lightly once, then again. The anxious whispering sounds stopped.

She kept caressing his head, whispering gentle sounds. Words didn't matter, she had learned, just the sounds. After a while, Zach began to relax. His fists came un-clenched. At last, he let out a long breath and drifted down into untroubled sleep.

With a sigh of her own, Kate watched the boy for several minutes longer, worried. Zach still suffered ter-ribly from the loss of his father a year ago, and continued to express his grief as anger and rebellion. He was like a train that had derailed, and his desperate mother had sent him to Camp Reliant in hopes that the counselors could help get him back on track again.

Kate had tried. She had given that effort all she had. But nothing had worked, and now she was feeling about as desperate as Mrs. Forrest.

I can't fail you, Zach, she thought. *I just can't.*

But she was so afraid that she would.

The next morning, Kate gathered up the clothes that she had worn exploring the caves with Gavin Buckley. Last night, she had left them draped over a chair in her room to dry. As she went through the pockets of her trail shorts before tossing them into the laundry basket with the sweatshirt that Gavin had loaned her, she felt something down at the bottom of one of the deep cargo pockets.

Digging it out, she moved over to the window to hold her hand in a shaft of bright sunlight. In the hollow of her palm lay a perfect cave pearl.

"Oh, rats!" she murmured. The cave pearl must have splashed into her pocket when she and Gavin fell into the pool of moonmilk. And without his actually having said so, she'd had the distinct impression that removing pearls from caverns was as much of a no-no as littering.

Kate carefully wrapped the pearl in a tissue and tucked it into a dresser drawer. She planned to give it to Gavin when . . . *if* they met again. Maybe he could return it to its rightful place in the cavern's rimstone pool.

She smiled wistfully at the memory of their accidental dunking. Gavin's startled laugher had reverberated off the cavern walls, mingling with her own. Kate had never had so much fun being cold, wet, and tired. But she had come to see her venture into the cave system as an isolated event in her life, not the first of a string of experiences. It was as if some hidden mechanism within Kate refused to allow her remarkable day with Gavin Buckley to become gilded with expectations.

Closing the drawer, Kate left her room and headed down the hallway toward the front door.

"Kate . . . you're just the person I want to see."

She halted near the door and turned to watch Cliff Peet limp down the stairway. When he reached the bottom, he held out a small white envelope.

"This is a key to the padlock up at the cave," he said. "You said last night that the Buckley fella had locked the gate when you left. You'd better run the key into town to him, or he won't be able to get into the cave system to do his mapping."

"But—"

"No buts, Kate." Peet scowled at her, but she couldn't miss the playful glint in his eyes. "It's the least you can do after Buckley saved you from drowning and all."

Kate rolled her eyes and took the envelope. "I knew I shouldn't have told you about that." Drowning, indeed. The pool of moonmilk had been only inches deep.

"I phoned ahead and got instructions to Buckley's office," he said. "They're right there on the back of the envelope, so get on with you. And be back by two-thirty. We'll need you to supervise the middle leg of the obstacle-course run this afternoon."

Two-thirty? Kate watched Peet go out the front door and clomp down the steps. He was giving her half the day off work without her even asking. What was going on here?

Kate was still standing there wondering about that when Lana came skipping down the stairs. When she spotted Kate, she actually smiled.

"Toby and I are teaming up on the animal-tracks class this morning," Lana said, and followed her father out the door.

Ah, Kate thought, understanding why Lana was so uncharacteristically cheerful. Any chance to work side by side with Toby Harris just naturally made the girl's day. Unfortunately, Kate was certain that Lana's feelings weren't shared by Toby.

Kate tucked the envelope containing the key into the pocket of her denim skirt and trailed after both of the Peets.

* * *

Mark poured two mugs of coffee and plunked both down on the conference table before sagging into one of the plush swivel chairs near Gavin. Both men propped their boots up on the same corner of the table. Gavin cradled a mug and stared out the broad expanse of windows, though he didn't appear to be looking at either the nearby stream or the woods beyond.

With his back to the windows, Mark had only Gavin to stare at. He couldn't say that he enjoyed the view.

"You have a problem today, bud?" Mark asked.

Gavin gave him a distracted look. "Hmm?'

"You haven't said three words since you came through that door a while ago. What's eating at you?'

"Nothing." Gavin shook his head. But he still looked distracted, as if he weren't in that room at all.

"All right, if you say so." Mark peered down into his mug. The coffee was truly awful, but he had no one to blame but himself, because he had brewed it. He hooked a thumb toward the door to the reception area, and said, "You'd think the new temp would pitch in with the coffeepot. She's bound to come up with something less disgusting than this."

"Don't rock that boat. She agreed to come down here and help out while Mickie's regular receptionist is on vacation. But she drew the line on domestic chores." Gavin rolled his eyes toward the door. "I about got thrown out of the building yesterday when I suggested some home-baked cookies might be nice."

"Sheesh!" Mark thought about that for a moment. "What kind?"

"Chocolate chip."

"The chewy kind?"

Gavin nodded. "They're her specialty."

"Really?" Mark pursed his lips. "You think maybe—"

"Not a chance. She says she's a receptionist this week, period. So unless you want to get Mickie on your case for driving off her temp worker, don't rock the boat."

They dropped the subject of cookies, though their brief trip down that road had somehow made the coffee taste even worse, which wasn't easy. Mark sighed, wondering idly if Butterfly was any great shakes as a cook—then found that he didn't care.

But that did serve as a reminder. He drained his mug, then set it aside and reached into his shirt pocket. "I need a favor."

Gavin drew his gaze from the window again as a small box tied with gold elastic string came skidding across the table at him. "What's this? You're giving me presents?"

Mark snorted. "In your dreams. I need you to deliver that out to Camp Reliant for me."

"Who's it for?"

"The redhead with the butterfly tattoo. I don't know her name."

"You don't know her name, but you're sending her presents."

"Come on, Gav." Mark gave his friend's boot a neighborly kick. "I can't get my mind off her. Give me a hand, will you?"

Gavin hefted the box, testing its weight, and then returned it to the table. "You can take it out there as easily as I can."

Mark delivered another kick, this one not quite so neighborly. "You know that isn't how this works."

They both frowned at the box, worrying at it from different sides of the fence.

Finally, Gavin picked it up and crammed it into his

pocket. "You're a trick, Mark. But I've always admired your imagination."

A slow grin bled across Mark's lips. "Now tell me, what's bugging you?"

"I told you, nothing."

"Nothing's name wouldn't be Kate O'Riley, would it?"

Gavin cast a sideways look at his friend. It wasn't the least bit neighborly. "If I'm going to be your delivery service," he said, "you'd better pour me some more of this pitiful excuse for coffee."

"My pleasure."

The sun was out, and so were the wildflowers. Spiderwort and Queen Anne's lace rioted alongside the highway, creating dazzling splashes of purple and white in the bright midsummer sunlight. Kate hummed to herself, enjoying the rush of balmy air through the open windows of the Camp Reliant van as she sped eastward toward White Sulphur Springs.

The instructions that Cliff Peet had scrawled on the envelope were easy to follow. She turned off the highway just as traffic began to thicken as she neared the resort area, and followed a winding macadam road for half a mile. The road led her to Doe Meadow, a circle of cedar-shingled single-story office buildings nestled in a densely wooded valley. The complex looked rustic in an exclusive sort of way.

A great place to work if you can get it, she thought.

She parked in front of a building bearing a big wooden number four on the front, and got out. Scattered around the parking lot were two dozen other vehicles, ranging from a flashy little Mercedes sports car to the yellow Hummer that Mark had driven out to Camp Reliant to pick up Gavin the other day. Despite all the vehicles, the office complex seemed secluded from the rest of the world.

A flagstone walkway led up to the beveled-glass door to Number Four. To the left of the door was a brass plate engraved with BONNER ENTERPRISES. Recalling that the lawyer who represented the owner of the cave system near Camp Reliant was named Bonner, Kate pulled open the door.

The reception area had dark-red carpeting, and comfortable upholstered chairs arranged in pairs around small tables decorated with colorful tile mosaics. An antique cherrywood desk angled across the back-left corner. Behind the desk, a dignified looking gray-haired woman in an aquamarine linen suit sorted neat stacks of mail.

She looked up as Kate entered. "May I help you?"

"I'm not sure." Kate stepped up to the desk, holding up the envelope containing the key to the cave-system gate. "I'm supposed to deliver this to a geologist named Gavin Buckley. Does he work here?"

The woman raised a brow and took a closer look at Kate, then smiled. Kate didn't quite know what to make of that smile. It looked suspiciously as though the woman had a private joke going.

"Yes." The woman nodded slowly. "Yes . . . I can see."

Kate grew uneasy, wondering exactly what it was that the woman could see. The longer she stood there, the more strongly she sensed that she was being subjected to some kind of make-or-break visual examination. The feeling was unsettling, to say the least. And yet, there was also something warm and appealing about her examiner.

The woman waved a manicured hand toward a paneled door to her left. "Go right on in," she said, as friendly as could be.

Kate eyed the door, suddenly wary. The woman kept on smiling, as if daring her to enter. "Uh . . . I could just leave the key with you." But she didn't really want to miss a chance to see Gavin one last time—assuming, of course, that he was on the premises.

"No, no." The woman made impatient little shooing motions with her fingers. "Go on in."

"Well . . . if you're sure."

Kate went to the door and raised a hand to knock. The woman shook her head, again making that shooing gesture. So Kate relented.

The door opened into a spacious room with a window-wall that looked out onto a rushing stream backed by lush woods. Another wall was covered with what appeared to be geological maps. A large oak conference table dominated the center of the room.

At the far end, Gavin Buckley and Mark Eisly sat with their boots propped on the oval table, cradling man-size ceramic mugs. When they saw Kate, two sets of boots came down fast.

"Well, hi there," Mark said with a delighted smile.

Gavin looked surprised, the warm glint in his eyes somehow even more welcoming than Mark's greeting.

Both men stood, Gavin looking frozen in place. Mark shot a bemused glance at him, then pulled out another of the high-backed swivel chairs.

"What brings ya, Kate?" he asked. "Can I get you a cup of coffee?"

Kate waved off the chair. "No thanks. I'm just here on an errand."

"Good choice. The coffee stinks."

She held out the envelope. "This is the key to the padlock on the gate. Cliff Peet wanted to make sure you could get into the cave system when you needed to work there."

Mark arched a brow, much as the receptionist out front had. He made no move to accept the envelope.

Just as Kate was beginning to feel awkward, holding out the envelope to no takers, Gavin brushed past Mark and scooped it out of her hand. The fleeting brush of his fingers across her palm brought a reflexive smile to her lips.

A smile that Gavin mirrored.

"Why, Kate, you didn't need to drive all this way to deliver that," Mark drawled, casting a sidelong glance at Gavin. "Buckley here was planning to head out to Camp Reliant to fetch it."

"Mark," Gavin said easily without taking his gaze off Kate, "get lost."

The hydrologist laughed, clapped Gavin on the back, and headed for the door. He had his hand on the knob when he stopped and turned back.

"Say, Kate," he said. "You know that butterfly you were with that time we came across you hiking on the mountain trail?"

Butterfly? It took Kate a moment to realize he was referring to Lana and her tattoo. "Her name is Lana Peet," she said.

"Lana." He seemed to savor the name. "Well . . . could you take her something for me?"

"Sure."

"Great." Mark held out his hand to Gavin, waggling his fingers. "Gav was going to take it for me, but since you're here . . ."

Gavin pulled a flat box about half the size of a deck

of cards from his shirt pocket. He tossed the box to Mark, looking relieved to be rid of it. Mark passed it to Kate.

"There's a note inside," he said.

Kate was more than a little intrigued. "Don't worry, Mark. I won't peek." But her curiosity itched maddeningly. "You could take it yourself, you know."

Gavin muttered something under his breath that Kate didn't quite catch.

Mark ignored him and nodded at Kate. "Yeah, I could do that." He gave her a playful wink and opened the door. "By the way, Kate—how are you with chocolate-chip cookies . . . the chewy kind?"

She gave him a blank look, not getting his drift.

"Eisly . . ." Gavin growled.

Mark laughed and ducked out of the conference room. When Kate looked at Gavin, he was slowly shaking his head at the closing door.

"Cookies?" she said, puzzled.

"Never mind."

She gave up on figuring out the cookie remark, and fingered the box again. "How odd, his wanting me to deliver this. Mark doesn't strike me as the shy type."

That seemed to strike Gavin as funny. "Oh, Mark isn't shy. He just believes women find the written word more irresistible than the spoken word. In Butterfly's case"— he shrugged—"it was fascination at first sight. He wants to make a good early impression before he beats a path to her doorstep."

That news almost backed Kate up a step.

"Now my curiosity really is killing me." She went so far as to shake the box. Then she lowered her voice. "But I have to say, Lana thinks Mark is too short."

Gavin threw back his head and laughed—a deep, rich

sound. He said, "Kate, let me tell you something about Mark Eisly. I've known him for eight years, and the last time it even occurred to me that he was short was the day we first met. Once Lana Peet gets to know him, she'll learn how little a person's height matters."

"You sound like the two of them getting chummy is a foregone conclusion."

He nodded. "When Mark sets his mind to something, he's a very dedicated man. And like I said, when it comes to Butterfly, he was a goner at first sight."

Maybe so, Kate thought. But Mark didn't know about Lana's crush on Toby Harris. Nor was he aware that the young woman sometimes could be . . . well, difficult to be around.

"Still," she said, "I wish I'd had a chance to talk to him about this." She turned the box over, noticing that besides being secured with gold elastic string, it had been taped shut. Insurance, she thought, remembering that Gavin had been the intended delivery service. Fingering the tape, she said, "I don't think Mark trusts you."

Gavin nodded. "He doesn't want me stealing his precious prose."

"Oh?" Kate tilted her head. "You write love letters?"

His gaze locked with hers, and for an instant Kate regretted her sauciness—but only for an instant. Then she felt a warm, increasingly familiar flutter as something deep inside her stirred and took wing.

When Gavin finally broke eye contact with Kate, he gazed down into his coffee mug, frowning. When he spoke, there was an odd hoarseness in his voice. "Kate, Mark makes the worst coffee in the world. What do you say we get out of here and see if we can find a decent brew someplace?"

She could tell that coffee was just an excuse, and that

getting out of the office—with her—was his true objective. The flutter returned. She didn't understand how the man could make her so nervous, and yet leave her with the feeling that she could lean on him if she needed to, and that he would never let her down.

She reminded herself that they'd known each other for only a few days. You couldn't possibly get to know a man so well in that short a time.

Not unless you've fallen into moonmilk with him.

"There's a little café up on the highway," she suggested.

He gave her a crooked grin. "Then let's give it a spin."

Gavin escorted her out of the conference room. As they crossed the reception area, the gray-haired woman at the desk glanced up from her mail sorting. She looked at Kate, then at Gavin, her eyes shining.

"Have a real nice morning, hon," she said sweetly.

Gavin pointed a warning finger at her, glowering menacingly. But then he said as politely as a schoolboy, "You, too, Aunt Lil."

The Grist Mill Café sat just off the highway east of the Doe Meadow turnoff. Built of weathered fieldstone with a green-shingled roof, the structure sported a working mill wheel driven by the mountain stream that ran along one side of the building. The wheel made a rhythmic creaking, thudding sound as it turned. Long strands of dripping, spring-green moss draped the paddles, glistening in the sunlight.

Inside, the café smelled of fresh-baked breads and cinnamon. An old-fashioned lunch bar ran across the back wall. Square oak tables filled the rest of the dining room, with booths along the front wall. Hand-woven bread baskets hung from the exposed rafters. There weren't many customers at that hour of the morning. There were, in fact, only two.

Kate sat across from Gavin in a cozy corner booth. They hadn't spoken much since ordering their coffee. The steady creak-thud of the water wheel had a lulling effect that seemed to fill the need for conversation.

She watched Gavin methodically doctoring his coffee, adding cream and sugar, then stirring. The shiner that she had given him at their first meeting was fading. She had an urge to reach across the table and touch the discoloration, to trace her fingertips across the tender skin beneath his eye. But not even the moonmilk had made her that bold.

"Was that really your aunt back at the office?" she asked, still not understanding why the woman had given her such a once-over.

Gavin shook his head with a long-suffering sigh, but then nodded. "My sister was desperate to find a temp for her vacationing receptionist. Aunt Lil agreed to fill in— she does enjoy being at the center of the action where she can meddle." He shook his head again, but Kate didn't miss the fondness in his voice.

"Your sister manages Bonner Enterprises?" she asked.

"Mickie *is* Bonner Enterprises. My brother-in-law's law firm helped her out with some legal footwork when she was first going into business on her own. That's how they met. Now she heads an investment group that owns the property where the caverns are located."

"No kidding? They own a whole mountain?"

His brow wrinkled. "When you put it that way, it does sound kind of awesome, doesn't it?"

"Definitely. So that's what brought you down here to map the cave system?"

"That and the caves themselves. An entire uncharted

cavern system was too good to pass up. I'm doing the mapping at cost. Mickie thinks she's getting a fantastic bargain, but I happen to believe that I'm the one who's getting the great deal."

Kate rested her chin on her hand, considering Gavin Buckley and his twin sister. "Wow—a successful businesswoman and a professor in the same family. Besides being a high achiever, is your sister like you?"

Gavin raised his cup and took a long swig of coffee, watching Kate. When he lowered the cup, he was smiling. "Oh, I don't know. What am I like?"

Good-looking, she wanted to say. *Intelligent. Fearless. Fascinating.* She settled on, "Adventurous. A risk-taker."

His brow furrowed again. "I suppose Mickie qualifies as adventurous. To celebrate her graduation from college, she bungee-jumped off a bridge up in Washington State. Before getting married, she spent a couple of years in the Peace Corps in East Africa. She's hiked about half of the Appalachian Trail . . . so far. Last May, she rode her horse in a seventy-five-mile endurance race—came in second, and is determined to bring home the gold next time. Her husband, Carl, says it's like being married to a three-ring circus."

Mickie Bonner sounded like one intimidating woman. Kate said, "So . . . one of you actually believes in marriage."

If she could have eaten her words, Kate would have chowed down on those in a heartbeat, but it was too late. Gavin's expression closed up like a shuttered window, and what had been a pleasant conversation became a vacuum.

He drank his coffee and stared out the window at the intermittent traffic on the highway out front. Kate toyed with her coffee cup, picking it up, setting it down, turning it left and then right in its saucer. When she could stand it no longer, she said, "I'm sorry."

His eyes widened slightly, but he kept his gaze on the highway. "What on earth for?"

Now Kate was stuck with trying to explain herself. "The other day, you made it clear how you feel about marriage. I shouldn't have made a joke about it."

Gavin finally looked at her. At first, that made Kate more uncomfortable than ever. But then his smile returned, warm and gentle as a summer breeze. "Kate O'Riley," he said, "you're an interesting woman."

Nobody had ever called Kate interesting before, and she certainly had never thought of herself in those terms. And the intent way he was looking at her was exciting in a way that was still new to her.

She wanted to ask what made her interesting to a man like Gavin Buckley. But she was afraid that he hadn't really meant it, and a lame answer would have been worse than none at all.

"How's Zach doing?" he asked out of the blue.

"Oh . . . fine," she said, caught off guard. He waited, obviously expecting more. Mentally scrambling, she added, "Gavin, Camp Reliant has a policy against discussing individual kids with anyone other than their parents."

He nodded, accepting that. "I pretty much know how he must be doing anyway."

That puzzled Kate until it occurred to her that Zach Forrest and Gavin Buckley had been about the same age when they suffered traumatic loss—Zach from the death of his father, and Gavin from the loss of both parents following their divorce. As far as Kate knew, Gavin hadn't been told about Zach's loss. Nevertheless, he seemed to have sensed that his own childhood shared common ground with the boy.

Kate didn't have to remind herself that Gavin was a university professor. His ability to empathize with a child he barely knew was astonishing. Without thinking, she started to reach across the table and touch his hand. Catching herself just in time, she drew her hand into her lap.

"I've been thinking over what you told me," he said, "about how the program at Camp Reliant helped you when you were a kid. I guess I could have used something like that when I was going through a rough spell."

"You seem to have done all right without it."

"Eventually," he said. "I've been thinking about that too. About how I didn't begin to get my head screwed on straight until I got hooked on caving."

Kate nodded. "Sometimes that's all it takes—an outside interest that seizes a child's imagination."

"Or a man's," he said softly, looking at Kate in a way that made her breath catch in her chest.

She glanced away, suddenly confused.

Gavin cleared his throat, as though acknowledging that the conversation had veered off course. "Listen, Kate, I had a talk with Mickie early this morning." He tugged a tightly folded sheet of paper from his pocket. "I was planning to drive out to Camp Reliant in the next day or so to bend Cliff Peet's ear. But since you're here . . ."

He shoved their coffee cups aside, unfolded the paper, and smoothed it flat on the table, anchoring two of the corners with salt and pepper shakers. Kate leaned over and studied a detailed topographical map.

"This looks like a miniature of one of the wall maps back at Bonner Enterprises," she said.

"You have a sharp eye."

On closer examination, she realized the map covered the county they were in. Half a dozen tiny red circles were clustered in the lower left quadrant.

"This is Camp Reliant," he said, pointing out an area filled in with yellow highlighter ink. He shifted his finger slightly to a red circle. "And this is the cavern entrance that Cliff Peet sealed off."

"What are these others?" Kate indicated the nearby red circles.

"Those are all cave entrances."

She rocked back. "So many?"

"Yup. They're all on Bonner property. And because they're so close to Camp Reliant, they're all in the process of being sealed off. Today, as a matter of fact."

Kate blew out a breath through pursed lips. "That's good to hear. I had no idea that mountain was so . . ."

"Riddled?" Gavin nodded. "Exciting for cavers, but kids don't need to be exploring there without supervision. And that's what I want to talk to you about."

His angular features animated with enthusiasm, he reached out and covered the hand that Kate hadn't tucked under the table. He didn't seem to realize what he had done, or that his warm, electric touch sent his excitement jittering through her as if she were plugged into some invisible power source.

"Do you remember telling me that the Camp Reliant program doesn't help all the kids who sign up?" he asked.

"That's right. No program anywhere does."

"So maybe the Camp Reliant program needs to expand—seek new horizons."

His fingers curled around Kate's, making it difficult for her to think straight. So she stayed focused on Gavin's eyes, allowing herself to be carried along by his passion for whatever it was he was getting at.

"We know Zach has been up there to that cave on his own," he continued. "We found his whistle there yesterday."

She nodded. "Thank heaven he can't do that anymore."

"But that's just it. Maybe shutting out Zach and kids like him isn't the answer." Gavin had both hands around hers now. "What if Camp Reliant had a caving program? The temperature in the caves never changes no matter what outside conditions are like, so you could have winter programs there too." He smiled. "No more rain-outs either."

Kate certainly liked the sound of that.

"It would give kids like Zach an adventure," he said. "Something to grab hold of and sink their imaginations into."

His grip on her hand tightened. Kate found that she was squeezing back, her pulse racing.

"But Camp Reliant has no one qualified to supervise such a program," she said. "None of us has any experience with caving."

"You have a start." Gavin tilted a wry grin. "I distinctly recall swimming in moonmilk with you."

Wading was more like it, but Kate wasn't about to split hairs. Not with her hand entwined with Gavin's. Swimming—wading—what difference did it make? What mattered was that she'd had fun exploring the heart of a mountain, discovering the magic and majesty of its silence.

Her mind took hold of his proposal and ran with it.

When Gavin was a boy, caving had provided a doorway leading out of an emotional wilderness. Maybe he was right—maybe supervised cave exploration could show other kids a way out of the wilderness too. Kids like Zach.

"But supervisors aren't a problem, Kate. Mickie already has her mind made up—Bonner Enterprises will definitely develop that cavern system for tourists. There'll be plenty of experts around to teach Camp Reliant counselors the ropes." He shrugged. "I wouldn't mind doing that myself. I could come down between semesters."

Kate liked the idea of Gavin paying return visits to the area. She was seriously attracted to him, no doubt at all about that, and she had a feeling that her feelings were reciprocated. But she knew better than to entertain wild fantasies about a deeper relationship developing between them—certainly not one that included marriage. Gavin had already made where he stood on matrimony crystal clear.

Still, she would look forward to seeing him now and then. It would be so nice to sit like this again, her hand lying warmly in his, her heart about to burst with excitement. That was something to hold onto.

"So, what do you think?" he asked. "Will Cliff Peet go for the idea?"

Kate hesitated, trying to put herself into her boss's shoes. As a rule, Mr. Peet was willing to try almost anything that might help even one child who was hurting. But he was also stubborn, and didn't appreciate outside interference.

"It's worth a try," she said. "Why not come back to Camp Reliant with me and talk with him about it?"

"Maybe this evening. You go ahead and fill him in, and I'll have more details for him later."

Kate's mind was racing. Even if Cliff Peet went for the idea, it would take months to set up a caving program at Camp Reliant, maybe as long as a year or more. But Zach Forrest would be gone in less than a week, and that saddened her. She couldn't shake the sense that she was badly failing Zach and not measuring up as a counselor.

As painful as that was to swallow, she had already begun to accept it.

Despite her growing sense of frustration, Kate tried to look at the brighter side. With Gavin's idea, maybe other counselors could help other troubled kids.

Gavin had come through. He had identified with Zach's pain, and that had driven him to come up with a plan of action that had the potential to make a real difference. If her boss could be convinced to give the proposed caving program a try, then at least Zach's misery might stand for something more than Kate's counseling had.

"Hey," Gavin whispered.

She looked across the table at his blurred features, realizing with some surprise that she had tears in her eyes. The smile that she forced felt crooked, and caused a tear to escape down her cheek.

Gavin caught it on the back of a finger, his eyes dark with concern. "Hey, what is it, Kate?"

"I was just thinking about what a terrific counselor you could be," she said. "You're a natural."

"What makes you think so?"

"Easy. You haven't forgotten what it feels like to be a child."

The warmth in his smile made her throat tighten. "Oh,

no, Katie O'Riley, you're wrong. I'd never have the nerve to step into your shoes. I'm not half wise enough."

She laughed, not believing a word of it, and more tears spilled out, embarrassing her. Gavin brushed at them again, the backs of his fingers barely kissing the flushed curve of her cheek.

As if on its own, her hand reached out and her fingertips lightly traced the fading bruise beneath Gavin's left eye. The tiny muscles there twitched, and she heard him catch his breath. She caught her own breath as his gaze dove into hers.

She knew then.

No doubt about it.

She'd made a terrible mistake. She was falling in love with a dream.

Chapter Five

Intermittent sunlight glinted off puddles along the obstacle course as fluffy rafts of mint-white clouds scudded across a manganese-blue sky. Kate perched high up on the crossbeam atop the rope-netting obstacle, waiting for the stragglers to arrive at the final obstacle.

There were two who hadn't yet completed the run—Tommy Reyes and Zach Forrest. The rest of the group, with Annie Rich in the lead as usual, had already scrambled over the obstacle and headed back to camp for a cookout supper.

From her perch, Kate fancied that she could smell the barbecue all the way from camp. That was just her imagination. All she could actually smell in the muggy air was the earthy odor of leaves and pine needles rotting on the forest floor after another all-night rain.

Shading her eyes against the sun, she spotted movement through the trees some distance down the obstacle-course trail. Tommy Reyes came struggling up the slope, arms pumping hard, trying to run in spite of his obvious fatigue. But he wasn't moving much faster than Zach

Forrest, who was walking along behind as if he were out on a Sunday stroll.

As the pair progressed toward the rope-netting obstacle, Toby Harris came into view, bringing up the rear. The senior counselor kept his distance from the boys, allowing them to move along at their own pace. But Kate could just imagine how aggravated he must be by Zach's total lack of motivation.

Tommy Reyes chugged up the slope, the little engine that could, arms flailing. Even at a distance, Kate could see how red his face was. She wanted to call down to him to take it easy, nobody had a stopwatch on him, he could take all the time he needed. But she was sure Toby had already told him that, probably repeatedly.

When Tommy reached the foot of the obstacle, he stopped to catch his breath, hanging onto the heavy rope netting for support.

"Don't start up until you're good and ready, Tommy," Kate said from atop the crossbeam. "I'm really proud of your effort today."

He grinned up at her, out of breath. "Thank you . . . Miss O'Riley. I'll do . . . even better . . . next time."

She laughed and gave him a thumbs-up. In five and a half weeks, Tommy had blossomed from a painfully shy child into a real competitor. Only his small size kept him from placing higher than last place on the obstacle course.

Kate was just thinking that Tommy had only one more chance to improve on that standing before the end of the midsummer program Saturday, when she was distracted by Zach Forrest. Ten feet from the base of the obstacle, he suddenly broke into a sprint and hit the rope-netting running.

Tommy froze, gaping and wide-eyed, as Zach scampered up the netting with the agility of a spider monkey.

"Slow down, Zach!" Kate moved quickly into position so she could lend a hand if he slipped.

But Zach reached the crossbeam, swung his body over the top without breaking his rhythm or so much as glancing at her, and flew down the other side.

"Man!" Tommy said, his expression ablaze with admiration.

Back on the ground, Zach slowed to a walk again and ambled out of sight up the trail.

Kate glanced toward Toby in time to see him throw up both hands in despair. All she could do was shake her head. Camp Reliant stressed sportsmanship and unity. But all Zach seemed to care about was showing what a better athlete he could be than his fellow students—if he wanted to be.

Which he never did.

"Miss O'Riley?" Tommy asked.

She looked down at the boy, still clinging to the bottom of the rope netting almost directly below her. "Yes, Tommy."

"Do you think I'll *ever* be good enough to make it over this obstacle as fast as Zach?"

"Not this one, Tommy," she said honestly, "because you'll be running the course only one more time—just three days from now, at the end of your program. But that doesn't mean you won't someday be just as fast as Zach, if that's what you want and you work hard at it."

"Oh, I'll work really hard," he said with enthusiasm, and started up the rope netting.

By the time Tommy approached the crossbeam, Toby had arrived at the base of the obstacle. He waited there, Kate was glad to see, in case the boy slipped. After five and a half weeks, Tommy still wasn't entirely sure-footed on the wobbly ropes.

"Watch where you put your feet," Kate reminded the boy. Because he always trailed the pack, Tommy often made climbing errors in his haste to catch up. "Remember—slower is faster if you don't make mistakes."

"That isn't what Zach says."

Kate waited until he reached the crossbeam before she stopped him and asked, "What does Zach say?" Knowing how much Tommy looked up to Zach, she was half afraid to hear his answer.

Tommy swung a leg over the top and straddled the crossbeam, facing Kate. "Zach says nobody ever won anything by being careful."

"Oh? And what do you think of that?"

He looked puzzled, as if it had never occurred to him to question his hero's opinions. "Well, I think . . . I think if you go around looking at your feet all the time, it might . . ."

When he didn't finish, Kate prodded him. "It might what?"

"It might be kinda . . . boring."

Kate wiped her palms down her thighs, thinking fast. "Tom, what is risk?"

"It's not being careful."

"Right. So tell me, how much risk is too much?"

He frowned, scratching his head. Kate waited patiently. For such a little guy, Tommy Reyes was a serious thinker once he put his mind to something.

"Too much risk," he said at last, "is when you do something really stupid?"

Kate nodded, hoping the boy kept that in mind, balancing good judgment against questionable advice. She remembered the whistle and lanyard she and Gavin

Buckley had found inside the cave yesterday. Zach's solitary and unsupervised adventures clearly had reached the level of too much risk. Fortunately, the padlocked gate at the cave's entrance had at least put an end to Zach repeating that trespass.

"What say we get back to camp and chow down on that barbecue?" she said. The smell of food was no longer her imagination, and it was growing stronger by the minute.

"Cool!" Tommy swung his other leg over the crossbeam and started down the other side. Kate accompanied him. "Miss O'Riley, did you really go way far into a cave with that guy yesterday?"

"That guy's name is Mr. Buckley," she said. "And where did you hear about that?"

"Everybody's talkin' about it."

"Well, yes. We did go way far into the mountain."

Tommy paused halfway down the rope netting and looked at her. "What was it like?"

"It was damp and chilly and darker than a moonless night." She smiled, thinking about the cathedral-like cavern . . . and the moonmilk. "And it was magical."

"But . . ." Tommy's eyes shone. "Wasn't going in there kinda, you know, risky?"

She shook her head, liking the way Tommy was following through with the premise. "Not very. Do you want to know why?"

He nodded.

"Because Mr. Buckley is an expert, so I was well-supervised. If I'd gone in there alone, not knowing anything about caves, that would've been risky " *Just like Zach,* she thought.

Tommy soaked that in for a moment, frowning. Then he said, "Gotcha," and continued on down to the ground.

Kate followed him down, hoping she really had gotten through to the boy. He was so in awe of Zach's recklessness. She worried that Tommy would try to emulate him.

Once the boy was on the ground, he trotted off toward camp. Kate waited for Toby to come around to her side of the rope climb, and they headed up to the compound at a slower pace.

"I started out with such high hopes for Zach," Toby said. "But I think I'm going to end up just wanting to wring his neck."

Kate glanced up at the senior counselor just to make sure he was joking. As aggravating and frustrating as Zach could be, they all knew the boy was hurting. Toby was just as anxious as Kate was to help him.

All those nights that she had soothed Zach out of his nightmares had kept her in touch with what lay beneath the difficult attitude. The angry, uncooperative child with whom they struggled every day was really just a scared kid running from his own pain.

"Kate, I'm afraid he might be a bad influence on Tommy Reyes. Tommy thinks Zach hung the moon."

"And yet," Kate said as she glanced back at the rope-netting obstacle, "when you think about it, look how Zach hung back so Tommy wouldn't have to finish the last leg of the obstacle course all alone."

Toby sucked on a tooth. "You sure that's why Zach was dragging his feet?"

She nodded, surprised by her own sudden conviction. "I would bet on it. However badly Zach behaves otherwise, he never lets Tommy down. Zach might be a real bundle of thorns on the outside, but inside he has a good heart. I just know it."

Toby smiled slightly. "Well, I'm glad I'm not the only

one who suspects that." They rounded a bend where the thin waterfall marked a fork in the trail, and started down a gentle slope toward the camp clearing. "By the way, Kate, you did a good job back there with Tommy, talking him through that risk business."

"Thanks." She could have hugged Toby for the compliment. But they both knew that Tommy Reyes was a relatively easy problem to solve. His main hang-up when he arrived at Camp Reliant had been a serious lack of self-esteem. The real hurdle that Kate needed to clear was Zach. After all, when it came to the crunch, it was the Zach Forrests of the world who were a true measure of a counselor's abilities.

But with only three days remaining in the current program, she was running out of time. So was Zach. And she still didn't have a clue as to how to reach him.

As if to underline Kate's own personal crisis of confidence, Cliff Peet came striding toward them from the camp compound. He did not look happy.

In his odd, limping gait, he stalked right up to them and halted, feet spread apart and hands clasped behind his back. Despite his age, he looked like a Marine Corps drill instructor reviewing a particularly disappointing platoon. Under his glare at that moment, Kate had never felt more like a raw recruit of particularly unpromising quality.

"Would you like to guess what just happened back there?" Peet cocked his head back toward the compound, where kids could be seen gathered around the picnic tables behind the main cabin.

Neither Kate nor Toby ventured a response.

"Well then, let me tell you," Peet said through clenched teeth. "Zach Forrest just came stampeding through the cookout and dumped a whole pot of mustard sauce on Annie Rich's head."

Kate's hand flew to her mouth. Toby groaned.

"Now I want to know what went on out there on the obstacle course to set him off . . . again," Peet said.

"Nothing that I know of." Kate glanced at Toby.

The senior counselor shrugged. "Zach was his usual self as far as I could tell, marching along to his own drummer, ignoring everybody else."

Cliff Peet scowled at them for a moment, and then seemed to deflate. "I don't know about that boy," he muttered. "I just don't know."

The three of them stood there at the foot of the trail for a minute or so longer, staring at their feet, pondering the difficulties presented by one twelve-year-old boy. Then Peet shook his head and snapped back into action.

"Toby," he said, "you'd best get on down there and supervise the cookout while Lana helps Annie Rich get that mess washed out of her hair."

"I'm on my way." Toby headed toward the compound.

Kate started to follow, but Peet stopped her with a look. She fidgeted, wondering what she was in for.

"We have a problem with that Forrest boy," he said, as if the obvious might have escaped her. "Between leaving camp unsupervised, and acting out the way he just did, well, what we're doing just isn't working for him."

"I've been worrying about that a lot."

"Then his mother called this morning. She's a real nice lady, and we had a long talk. Zach was out of control before she sent him up here. If we can't get him turned around, she says she might have to send him to a boys' home, and that's tearing her up." Peet rubbed the back of his neck. "The poor woman is worried out of her head that she's about to lose her only child."

Kate waited, hoping that he had a new strategy for her to try.

Instead, he said, "Zach's been troubled ever since he lost his father. The way I figure it, he isn't letting himself get close to people for fear he'll lose them too."

She nodded. Peet had already discussed that aspect of Zach's behavior with his camp counselors. But now he added another twist.

"I've been watching the boy, Kate. He's much more standoffish with Toby and me than he is with you. Maybe we men remind Zach more of the father he lost. So maybe—just maybe—you're the only one who has a chance of breaking through to him."

"But I've tried everything I can think of." Kate said in desperation. "Nothing has helped." Only when Zach was asleep, locked in a nightmare, was she able to calm his fears.

"I know you've given it your best shot. We all have." Peet let out a heavy sigh. "So it looks like we're going to need some high-powered magic."

Kate looked at him, wondering just how he expected her to pull a rabbit out of a hat. Before she could ask, he turned and trudged off toward the compound, hands still clasped behind his back. His head was down. From the slump in his shoulders, Kate could tell the prospect of failing a child made him heartsick.

A warbler trilled from a pine branch high overhead. Kate squinted up into the tree crown, thinking the cheerful song was totally at odds with her anguish over Zach.

Cliff Peet was right—nothing short of magic was going to turn Zach around with just three days remaining in the current program. But the only magic she had seen lately was the cavern that Gavin had shown her yesterday. And considering how Zach flouted Camp Reliant rules at every turn, Kate wasn't about to suggest that Peet allow the boy to venture into the cave system, even with supervision.

Just when her mood felt about as gloomy as it could get, a low rumble of thunder reverberated through the mountains.

As Kate crossed the clearing on her way to the main cabin a short while later, she ran across Lana Peet coming out of the girls' dorm.

"Did you get Annie cleaned up?" Kate asked.

Lana rolled her eyes. "That girl is mad enough to chew nails."

Not that anyone could blame Annie, Kate thought. "By the way, you're just the person I want to see. How about stopping by my room?"

"Can't," Lana said. "I have to go help with the cookout."

"This won't take a minute," Kate insisted, knowing the main reason Lana was so eager to return to work was so she could be near Toby Harris.

Lana looked put out, but followed Kate on across the clearing and into the main cabin. At Kate's room, she waited at the door, slouching with bored impatience, while Kate went to her dresser.

"Do you remember that hydrologist we met on the trail several days ago?" Kate asked. "The one who was hiking down the mountain with Gavin Buckley, name of Mark Eisly?"

"Sure. The short guy."

Yeah, well, according to Gavin, Mark is a lot taller than you think. "Mark sent you something."

"He did?" Lana looked as if she couldn't decide

whether to be amused, annoyed, or just plain baffled. "How come?"

"Isn't that obvious?" Kate smiled as she fished the small box from the top drawer of the dresser. "He's interested in you."

"Whoop-de-doo."

Wishing Lana didn't find it necessary to be so sarcastic, Kate waggled the box in the air. Lana came on into the room and accepted it from her.

"According to Mark, there's a note inside," Kate said.

Lana slipped off the gold-elastic string, broke the tape seal, and opened the end flap. She peeked cautiously inside as if the box might contain a tiny, venomous snake. Finding nothing threatening, she pulled out a tightly folded sheet of blue paper, which she unfolded. Obviously intent on making fun of Mark's offering she began to read aloud.

"Dear . . ." Lana stopped, her expression going quizzical. *"Dear . . . Butterfly."* Her hand went to the tattoo on the back of her shoulder as she continued:

I'm sending you something that's a million years old, because not in a million years will I ever forget your sea-green eyes and glorious red hair. I'm eternally grateful to you for filling my dreams with your beauty.

Mark Eisly

Kate bit her lips to keep from smiling as she watched Lana return to the top of the page and silently reread the note once, then again. Lana was frowning, but her cheeks had taken on a pink flush that made her downright pretty. The transformation was startling. Evidently, Lana had never received a love note before.

As if I have, Kate thought. She said, "Mark sounds rather taken with you, doesn't he?"

"Nobody ever told me I was—" Lana's voice choked off.

"Pretty?"

Lana nodded.

Studying the younger woman, Kate realized that a big part of being pretty was feeling pretty. And with just two sentences, Mark had managed to make Lana feel pretty indeed. She'd never seen a young woman undergo such a rapid change—certainly not on the basis of a few dozen words from a man whom Lana had previously looked down upon, both literally and figuratively.

Lana peeked into the box again, and used two fingers to tweeze out a wad of white tissue. Lips pursed, she carefully opened the tissue and plucked out a smooth, irregularly-shaped object about the size of her thumb, attached to a silver chain.

"A necklace." She fingered the pendant. "What *is* this?"

Kate leaned close to get a better look. "I'd say it's a sliver of polished limestone."

Lana dangled the pendant on its chain. "A rock?"

"A million-year-old rock."

"Hmm." Lana turned the pendant this way and that, as if she didn't know what to make of it.

Kate smiled, watching her. Mark Eisly had certainly gotten Lana's attention.

That the hydrologist was going to so much effort to make a good impression on Lana amazed Kate. He had seen something in Lana that not ever Kate had noticed— something that lay just beneath the surface. Kate wondered if that ability had come from all the time Mark had spent searching beneath the surface of the earth for deep, hidden waters.

Did exploring the very heart of a mountain and testing its ancient pulse make it easier for a person to see into the heart of a flesh-and-blood human being? Looking back, it seemed to Kate that during the magical hours that she had spent in the cavern with Gavin Buckley, he had reached right into her heart and thrown open a window. But a window to what?

To moonmilk, cave pearls, and . . . complicated possibilities.

From outside the cabin came a burst of young voices, reminding Kate that they had work to do.

She said, "We'd better lend Toby a hand with the cookout before the kids get rambunctious and duct-tape him to a tree."

At the mention of Toby Harris, Lana wadded the tissue around the pendant and crammed it back into the box along with Mark's note. She started for the door, halted abruptly, and then gave Kate a look of confusion.

"Should I, you know, like, call and thank Mark Eisly, or something?" Lana stammered, fingering the box.

Kate had never seen Lana so rattled, and the young woman had never asked her advice on anything before. Quite the contrary—Lana had always seemed to hold Kate's opinions in contempt. Two little sentences, Kate thought, had the power to shake Lana's world.

"I'm sure Mark would like a thank-you call," she said. "But I have a feeling you'll be seeing him quite soon anyway."

"Really?" Lana's cheeks flushed again.

Pretty, Kate thought again. *Lana really is pretty. Maybe not in a conventional way, but deep inside, which*

is the only place that counts. How could Mark Eisly have
seen at a glance what I've been blind to it all summer?

She smiled. "Really."

Lana rolled her eyes in a way that could have meant
anything, and ducked out the door.

As the sound of Lana's footsteps receded quickly
down the hallway, Kate felt a sinking sensation in the
pit of her stomach. If she could have overlooked so much
in Lana Peet, how much had she missed seeing in Zach
Forrest?

Chapter Six

Sometime after 10:00 that night, Kate eased open the screen door to the boys' dormitory and stepped outside. Zach's nightmare had been even more troubling than usual this time. He had finally settled down and stopped thrashing and muttering, and Kate had left him sleeping peacefully. But her sense of having failed him had grown stronger than ever, gnawing at her conscience like a nest of termites.

She dropped down off the steps and started across the clearing. Most of the lights in the compound were off. Everyone but Kate had packed it in early. Even when the rest of the staff had called it a day, she had known she wouldn't be sleeping much that night—not with Zach preying on her mind.

At the main cabin, the planks of the front steps creaked faintly as she climbed to the porch. Sleepless but tired, Kate had just reached for the screen-door handle when she heard a truck engine grinding up the driveway from the road. Wondering who on earth would be paying Camp Reliant a visit at such a late hour, she stepped back down off the porch and waited.

A dim wash of headlights flickered through the trees as the truck grew nearer. Then, just before the vehicle rounded the final curve, the engine stopped. Seconds later, the headlights blinked off.

Puzzled, Kate moved farther out into the clearing.

From down the driveway came a metallic thump that might have been a truck door closing. She stood there hugging herself in the mild night air, suddenly jittery at the idea that someone might be trying to approach the camp by stealth.

A few minutes later, she detected movement in the moon-shadows at the head of the driveway. The movement stopped, leaving barely an impression of an indistinct form superimposed on the shadows of the trees. Nervous, Kate held her ground, acutely aware of how clearly visible she was in the ghostly moonlight. For a long moment, she remained breathlessly still, watching the watcher.

Then the figure started toward her.

Kate took an uncertain step back toward the porch, tension prickling her flesh. Her pulse quickened—then leaped in relief as Gavin Buckley strode into the moonlight.

He seemed to drift toward her, his footsteps silenced by the thick layer of pine needles blanketing the clearing. When he stopped an arm's length in front of her, Kate saw that he was smiling.

Gavin glanced at the nearly darkened cabins. "I parked below," he said in an undertone. "I didn't know how early you folks called it a day."

"It's been a busy one. Just about everybody has gone to bed."

"But not the most important body, I see."

Kate laughed softly. "What is this? Did you and Mark kiss the Blarney stone?"

He grinned. "Ah . . . so Butterfly got her package."

"Yes. And you can tell Mark it made an impression."

"Good or bad?"

"Profound, is my guess."

"Okay. Mark will be satisfied with that . . . for now."

Over near the girls' dorm, a screech owl cried out in the night—a descending, wavering flute note. Some distance away, another owl answered. Both Kate and Gavin turned their heads, listening.

"It's kind of late to be out roaming," she said after a while.

"I got held up in a meeting this evening. I'd hoped to make it out here in time to discuss the possible caving program with Cliff Peet." Gavin shifted his feet, gazed up at the night sky, and then leaned closer to Kate. "But mostly, I wanted to see you."

She giggled nervously, which made her feel silly.

"So here I am," he said, "thinking it's late for you to be afoot when the whole camp has turned in."

Kate shrugged. Camp rules and her own discretion forbade her from telling Gavin about Zach's nightmares. "I couldn't get to sleep," she said. It wasn't precisely a lie. She hadn't actually tried to sleep, knowing ahead of time that there was no hope for it.

"Is that right?" Gavin rocked back on his heels, slid his hands into his pockets, and gazed up at the sky again, focusing this time on the bloated moon. The owl called out again, and was answered. "Then maybe I could interest you in taking a walk with me."

"In the dark?"

"Dark?" He grinned at her. "Why, this isn't dark,

Kate. Dark is when you can't see your hand in front of your face. You can practically read by the light of this moon."

"Maybe you can, Gavin Buckley. But I'm not used to spending my time in the belly of a mountain. Night is still plenty dark to me."

"Ah. Then perhaps what you need is some conditioning."

Gavin thrust out his elbow. The gesture seemed comically gallant under the circumstances. Kate couldn't resist sliding her hand around his arm. He placed his free hand over hers and they moved up the clearing toward the waterfall.

As they put the compound behind them, he said, "Katie O'Riley, what are you laughing about?"

"I'm sorry, I can't help it. This feels like . . . well, like we're a Victorian couple strolling in the park." *Me in my warm-ups and sneakers.*

"Well, now. I'm touched that you see us as a couple."

Kate felt herself blush in the dark—and it was quite dark, as they moved in and out of moon-shadows. This new tendency of hers to blush when she was around Gavin was beginning to get on her nerves. She was as bad as Lana Peet, who had turned ten shades of pink after reading Mark Eisly's note.

At the waterfall above the north end of the clearing, they were confronted by two separate trails. One led steeply to the right, and the other angled off to the left.

"That one goes up toward the cave, doesn't it?" Gavin indicated the trail to the right.

"Yes. And this other one leads to the obstacle course."

"You know, Katie, you haven't lived until you've had a midnight tour of a cavern."

"Oh, right. As if it's going to be any different in there

at midnight than at high noon." She tugged his arm, taking a firm step to the left.

"It's your call, Kate. But you don't know what you're missing."

"Uh-huh."

Something in Gavin's tone suggested romance. On any other evening, Kate might have been tempted. But concern over Zach Forrest had her too wound up for another adventure. Besides, she knew better than to let herself become too involved with Gavin.

As they moved up the trail, she wished she could talk about her problems with Zach. She had a feeling that Gavin would be supportive, and she could use a sturdy crutch right then. But rules were rules. Kate wasn't about to violate Camp Reliant's confidentiality regulations.

The trail to the left wound gently up through the trees. A soft breeze stirred the boughs overhead, sending the moon-shadows into a dancing frenzy.

A few minutes later, Gavin said, "What do we have here?"

Ahead, the rope-netting obstacle loomed against the greater darkness of the woods. "It's the final obstacle on the course."

"You don't say." Sounding intrigued, he released her hand and took hold of the heavy rope. "Will it support adults?"

"Sure."

"Then let's go."

Before Kate could object, Gavin sprang up the netting, moving effortlessly, reminding her so much of Zach that she held her breath. Seconds later, he was seated on the crossbeam, legs dangling, looking down at her.

"What's the hold-up, Kate?"

His mocking tone got her moving. Not to be outdone, Kate raced up the ropes.

"Hey, you're good," he said as she settled next to him on the crossbeam. "Looks like you've done this before."

"Only about a hundred times." She closed her eyes and raised her face toward the moon as if she were sunbathing. "But I've never been up here at night. This is nice."

"Yeah. You wouldn't think being just ten or twelve feet above the ground would make any difference. But the stars seem so much closer from up here."

Kate opened her eyes and reached a hand toward the star-dusted vault of the night sky. Another hand appeared next to hers, pointing.

"Look," he said. "Ursa Major. The Big Bear."

"Oh, forget that, Gavin. I never could see constellations. They're always just a jumble of stars to me."

"Wait." He pulled her close against him and pointed again. Kate peered down the length of his arm as he traced a finger across the sky, playing connect-a-dot with the stars that made up the Big Bear. "And just over there, Ursa Minor—the Little Bear. And right there, Polaris, the North Star."

Kate felt a thrill of excitement as she did at last see the sprawling constellations, though they were partially concealed by the treetops. Yesterday, Gavin had shown her the magic of caverns deep inside a mountain. Tonight he had handed her the magic of the universe.

"Amazing," she murmured.

"Yes . . . amazing," he said in a near whisper.

But when Kate glanced up at him, he wasn't looking at the sky. He was looking at her. And there it came again—the blush. Kate turned her head away, though she knew he couldn't have seen her face redden in the moonlight.

They sat for a long time, gazing up at the heavens, her head resting on Gavin's shoulder. Eventually, with his arm around her and the night breeze feathering her skin, Kate gave a deep sigh and relaxed. As the night drifted gently toward midnight, she wished they could remain like that forever.

And yet, it was Kate who finally broke the silence. "I forgot to tell you this morning. When I got back from the cavern, I found a cave pearl in my pocket. It must have gotten there when we fell into the moonmilk."

"So you ended up with a souvenir."

"No! I mean, I want you to take it back to where it belongs. I feel like an accidental thief."

Gavin traced a thumb lightly along the curve of her jaw. "We'll take it back together."

Kate nodded. She would like that. She'd be careful about making too much of their friendship, but she would enjoy another trip into the caverns. She found their hidden reaches surprisingly alluring.

He shifted his weight on the crossbeam. Kate started to move away, but he kept his arm around her, holding her snugly against his side.

"I guess I ought to explain why I was so late," he said. "The meeting that held me up this evening was with my sister. Mickie has been up in Boston all week. We had a long talk on the phone this morning, but this was the first chance we'd had to really sit down and discuss details of developing a caving program for kids when she opens the caverns to tourists."

"And?"

"Mickie is excited. She thinks a youth program would be a good draw for tourists. She's planning to drive out

here herself in the morning and talk with Cliff Peet."
When Kate made no comment, he nudged her. "I thought
that news would make you happy."

"Oh, it does. But . . ."

"Come on, Kate. Spit it out."

She had spent quite a while mulling over the prospect
of a caving program for the kids, trying to see it from
Mr. Peet's viewpoint. She could see one major objection
that he was bound to have. "Camp Reliant isn't just a
summer-activities camp, Gavin. Our kids have problems,
and we help them work through those."

"That's what I've gathered."

"So I don't think Mr. Peet will be interested in a caving program geared for tourists. Our kids would need
something more than that."

Gavin fell silent for a moment. Then, "So Mickie will
negotiate with him."

"You won't believe how stubborn Mr. Peet can be
when it comes to his kids."

He chuckled. "And *he* won't believe how persuasive
my sister can be when it comes to her enthusiasms."

Kate had been wondering what Gavin's twin looked
like. Now she envisioned a lady Marine in full combat
gear. Suddenly she didn't look forward to tomorrow
morning.

A stiff gust of wind rattled through the treetops, then
calmed. In the stillness, they heard industrious, shuffling
sounds below. Leaning over, they watched a fat raccoon
make a complete circuit of the obstacle, stopping every
few feet to sniff the air. Then it waddled off into the
surrounding woods. Another gust of wind stirred the
trees. The stillness that followed felt heavy and unsettled.

"Guess I'd better not keep you up all night," Gavin
said, though he made no move to leave their perch.

Instead, he turned her toward him and eased his fingers into her loose hair, his thumbs lightly brushing her cheekbones. His face was close, a peculiar look of wonder in his eyes.

The way he just held her there, gazing at her, made her dizzy. She closed her eyes, seeking balance.

His lips met hers with such aching tenderness that Kate gasped. For an eternal moment, she felt dreamily as if she could float right on up to the stars. And then his lips were gone.

Kate opened her eyes . . . to blindness.

"What . . . !" She clutched at Gavin's hands, startled. Then laughed in relief when she realized what had happened.

Clouds were rolling in, sending the Big and Little Dippers into hiding and obliterating the moonlight. The wind was getting up in earnest, bringing with it the smell of rain.

Gavin chuckled. "I think we've caused a change in the weather."

He pulled her into his arms. Kate instinctively wrapped her arms around him, and they remained there on the crossbeam for a moment longer, defying the wind, reluctant to leave.

Despite her best intentions, Kate was afraid she might be falling in love with Gavin Buckley, and that her feelings for him had just taken an irresistible turn. She had to remind herself that loving Gavin was a dead-end road. He had already made it clear that he was a no-strings-attached kind of man.

In the distance, a crack of thunder reverberated, sounding like a badly rolled ball bouncing down a bowling alley. That got them moving.

Gavin helped Kate off the crossbeam. But as they hurried down the rope mesh side by side, she felt a profound tug of regret. She was grateful for all the magic he had brought into her life. But she knew in a flash that she could not afford even the dream of Gavin Buckley. To love this man and lose him—even in her dreams—would break her heart beyond repair.

She knew that. But she couldn't seem to help herself.

Chapter Seven

All through breakfast, gray sheets of rain poured off the roofs of the cabins. At 9:00 sharp, the deluge ended as abruptly as a turned-off faucet. Minutes later, a tattered hole appeared in the clouds, admitting a brilliant shaft of sunlight. Raindrops dripping from the trees and cabin eaves glistened like jewels in the clean, sweet air.

The entire population of Camp Reliant poured out of the cabins to marvel at the rapidly clearing sky.

Kate had resigned herself to being marooned indoors with a dozen restless youngsters. Now as the clouds shredded and disintegrated before her eyes, she felt as giddy as the kids. Even Lana surprised everyone with a perfectly graceful somersault.

With just two days remaining before Saturday's close of the current program, Cliff Peet had scheduled an outdoor drill to test the kids' wilderness first-aid skills. Toby Harris had just sent the kids back to their dorms to fetch their first-aid manuals when a yellow Hummer ground its way up the driveway into the clearing.

The vehicle pulled up in front of the main cabin and

parked just feet away from where Cliff Peet and the three Camp Reliant counselors were standing on the porch. Three doors opened on the Hummer. Gavin Buckley and Mark Eisly emerged from the front. A tiny mahogany-haired woman in a royal-blue jumpsuit exited the back. She carried an oxblood-leather briefcase.

At the sight of Gavin, Kate drifted back to stand against the front wall of the cabin, though she wanted to do just the opposite. Their hours of stargazing last night had left her changed in fundamental ways. She wasn't sure if she could bear to be around Gavin now, knowing as she did that their relationship had no future beyond what it already was.

"Welcome to Camp Reliant," Mr. Peet said, stepping to the edge of the porch. "To what do I owe the pleasure?"

"I want you to meet my sister, Mr. Peet," Gavin said, ushering his companion up the steps. "Mickie has something she's itching to talk to you about."

Mickie Bonner bounded up the steps, radiating energy. Mr. Peet gave her a reserved, noncommittal smile as he shook her outstretched hand.

Gavin joined his sister on the porch, introducing her to Lana Peet, and then to Toby Harris. When they reached Kate, a small frown line appeared between the woman's wide-set eyes. She held onto Kate's hand as she gave her a long, hard once-over. And then Mickie smiled as though at a private joke, just as her Aunt Lil had the previous morning.

"You're everything my brother said you were." Mickie laughed.

Kate glanced past Mickie at Gavin. He seemed a touch embarrassed by his sister's remark. Mickie smiled innocently at him, leaving Kate with the impression that she was going out of her way to get her brother's goat.

Returning her attention to Kate, Mickie held her hand for several more seconds before giving it a parting squeeze that seemed oddly surreptitious.

Kate couldn't stop staring at Mickie as the woman turned back to Cliff Peet. In person, Gavin's sister certainly didn't look like a lady Marine. What was more, with the exception of their mahogany hair, the two couldn't have looked less like twins. Mickie had an olive complexion and small, delicate features. She wasn't much taller than the kids who were now bounding back out of their dorms across the clearing. And yet, there was a formidable steeliness about her narrow, straight back, and in the way she stepped right up to Cliff Peet and placed her small hand on his beefy arm.

Kate realized that she liked Mickie Bonner on sight.

"Mr. Peet," Mickie said, "I believe you know our Uncle Morgan up near Covington."

Cliff Peet nodded. "A fine fellow."

"I saw Uncle Morgan just last Tuesday. He said to give you his regards."

"That's neighborly," he said. "The same back to Morgan."

"My pleasure." Mickie patted his arm—a motherly gesture despite her being barely half his age. "Now how about if we go inside. You and I have some hash to fry."

He eyed her hand and the briefcase with suspicion. Kate had to admit she had never seen the man look so intimidated. From all appearances, Gavin was right about his sister being a force to be reckoned with.

"You see, Mr. Peet," Mickie was saying as the two disappeared inside, "I have this plan—"

The screen door slapped shut behind them.

"See what I mean about Mickie?" Gavin said. He stood on the bottom step with one boot propped on the porch, an elbow resting on his knee. "She's pure persuasion. Mr. Peet won't have a chance."

Kate glanced at Lana to see how she was taking her father's response to being steamrolled by Gavin's pint-sized sister. But Lana seemed to have more pressing distractions. Though Lana had positioned herself next to Toby, she seemed to be trying very hard not to look at Mark Eisly. She kept shooting furtive little glances his way.

Mark leaned casually against the Hummer, arms folded across his chest, openly sizing up Toby. Kate scratched her upper lip to cover a grin that she couldn't squelch. She wished she could tell Mark that Toby was no competition for him where Lana was concerned, except in Lana's mind. But then she decided that competition might be a good thing in this situation, even if it were imaginary.

Gavin caught Kate's eye and smiled. She smiled back, and then looked away, unable to cope with the warmth in his eyes.

All of the kids had spilled into the clearing, first-aid manuals in hand. The girls were gathering in an orderly knot in the center of the clearing, waiting for the counselors. Most of the boys had wandered over to peer through the tinted windows of the Hummer.

"Time to hit the trail," Toby announced, leading his fellow counselors down off the porch. "This break in the weather might not last long."

"Mind if we tag along?" Mark asked.

Toby looked from Mark to Gavin, who gave his friend a sidelong look. Mark flicked a split-second glance at Lana, and then looked angelically at Gavin.

Gavin gave a lazy smile of understanding, and said, "How about it, Toby? We promise to stay out of your way."

"No problem," Toby said. "The more the merrier. Maybe the kids will teach you some first-aid skills."

Some of the boys around the Hummer overheard their senior counselor and let loose a boastful cheer.

As Toby formed up the kids in a double row, preparing to lead them away from the compound, Lana moved over to where Mark was standing and spoke to him so softly that Kate couldn't quite make out what she said. Then to Kate's astonishment, Mark gave a courtly bow, took Lana's hand in his, and raised the backs of her fingers to his lips. Perhaps because Mark seemed dead-serious, the gesture didn't look nearly as absurd as it should have.

Lana's face went up in flames, and she fled to Toby's side.

"Is Mark making fun of her?" Kate murmured to Gavin.

"Never," he said in an undertone, sliding his hands into his pockets as he casually moved closer to Kate. "Mark's smitten, is what he is. And believe me, he's totally focused."

Gavin looked pretty focused himself, Kate thought nervously. The way he was looking at her, she might have been the only other person on the planet.

As the group moved out, Kate hurried to take up position in the rear, trying to put distance between herself and Gavin. But he remained at her side, carefully matching his longer stride to hers. She stared at the ground, the trees, the sky . . . anywhere but at Gavin.

"Should I warn Lana?" she asked, because not saying anything to him seemed louder than words.

"Come on, Kate," he protested quietly, "Mark's in love. Give him a fighting chance."

"Let me get this straight." She braved a sidelong glance at Gavin. "Your sister is back there steamrolling Mr. Peet, and your colleague is up ahead steamrolling Lana. You're alright with that?"

"Yup." He leaned close to whisper, "And I'm just moseying along wondering how in blue blazes I'm going to steal another kiss from the prettiest woman in all the Allegheny Mountains."

They had lagged a good ten yards behind the others. Kate couldn't have been gladder of that, because she could feel her entire body blush, from her sneakers to her hairline. This time it was broad daylight and Gavin couldn't help noticing—just as she couldn't help spotting the playful shine in his eyes.

"Gavin Buckley, as my grandmother would have said, you are a caution."

"Am I?" he said, with his sister's innocent smile. "Well, Katie O'Riley, you are a miracle."

Kate swallowed dryly. One hand came out of his pocket and brushed against hers. The sensation was jarring. It was all she could do to keep herself from reaching out to him. Instead, she picked up her pace and caught up with the others, thinking it was going to be a long morning if Gavin Buckley kept that close to her.

Toby led them to the midpoint along the obstacle course, where they gathered at the sandpit where many of Camp Reliant's outdoor classes were held, weather permitting. Rainwater had drained quickly out of the sand, making it less soggy than most other areas around camp.

Kate never did know just how the competition started—on a dare, probably. But whether the dare had come from Toby, Mark, or one of the kids, no one could say. One minute, she and Lana were supervising Annie Rich, who was demonstrating how to rig a makeshift stretcher out of T-shirts and a pair of saplings that the kids had cut. The next minute, every eye was turned toward the flag rope.

In the center of the pit, a twenty-foot rope as thick as a man's wrist hung from a long horizontal iron rod bracketed securely between two tall hickory trees. At the ten-foot point halfway up was affixed a red plastic flag, marking the topmost limit for Camp Reliant's youthful rope climbers.

Mark Eisly and Toby Harris stood next to the rope. Both had taken off their hiking boots, and Mark seemed to be indicating that Toby should go first.

"What's going on?" Kate asked.

"Oh, just some light chest beating," Gavin said. He was seated on a log nearby, fiddling with his watch. "One of them is going to walk away with bragging rights."

"To what?"

"To who's the fastest rope climber in these here mountains, ma'am," he drawled.

He cast a significant glance at Lana, who had moved to the edge of the sandpit to watch. Kate couldn't tell if Lana had any idea that the chest beating was for her benefit—at least, from Mark's standpoint.

The kids quickly abandoned their first-aid exercise to ring the sandpit, eager for a show. From the excited babble of voices, Kate gathered that fan support was leaning heavily toward Toby as the sure winner, a prejudice that she attributed both to camp loyalty and to their having witnessed the senior counselor's prowess on the obstacle.

But to her surprise, Tommy Reyes cast his vote for the short, dark interloper who had ridden in on the Hummer.

She glanced around for Zach, and spotted him standing off to one side, flipping pebbles at a tree and making a great show of ignoring the action.

Lana fingered a chain around her neck. Kate took a second look, and recognized the chain. She realized that Lana was wearing the pendant Mark had sent her, though the chip of polished limestone was hidden from view inside her T-shirt.

"Really," Kate said, keeping a watchful eye on the kids to make sure they stayed well away from the rope. "I thought guys outgrew this kind of behavior when they got out of high school."

Gavin chuckled. "Nope. We never do. Not when the stakes are sky-high."

"You know, Toby is really good on that rope."

"Uh-huh. Unfortunately, he's also built like a weight-lifter."

Kate moved over and leaned against a tree, wondering why Gavin seemed to think Toby's impressive muscles weren't an advantage.

She also wondered why Gavin wasn't over there in the sandpit preparing to show off his own proficiency with a rope. If his agility on the rope netting last night were any indication, she figured he could at least give both Mark and Toby some sporting competition.

Then the reason for Gavin's lack of interest in chest-beating hit her. Unlike Mark, he wasn't interested in winning a fair maiden. As he had said, Mark was smitten with Lana, had fallen for her on sight. But Gavin Buckley wasn't about to let himself fall in love with a woman. No, siree. He was a confirmed bachelor-for-life, and love and marriage were not in his future.

Her fingertips drifted to her lips as she recalled last night's kiss—the dizzying sensation that she could fly. One kiss, one brief eternal kiss, had changed her. Now, deep in her heart, she knew what could have been if the bitter divorce of Gavin's parents hadn't made him so wary of risking commitment.

One kiss.

Oh, Lordy, she thought. *Nothing hurts like a one-sided love. It's like half a circle, which is nothing at all.*

Gavin got up from the log and leaned against her tree trunk, close enough to touch if either of them moved mere inches. "What's the problem, Kate?" he asked in an undertone.

"Nothing."

"I know better. You've been trying to leave me in your dust ever since I got here this morning."

Kate shook her head. She couldn't talk to him about it, wouldn't even have known where to begin. And even if she wanted to, the time and place couldn't have been worse. Instead, she pointed toward the sandpit where Toby had taken hold of the rope.

Gavin glanced over there just in time to check his watch as Mark shouted, *"Go!"*

Toby started up the rope, hand over hand, making it look as easy as walking down a street. The kids surrounding the sandpit raised their voices in one collective scream of encouragement. Kate spared a quick glance at Lana, who had her fists clenched on either side of her head and was hopping up and down in place.

In a smooth, steady rhythm of hands and feet, Toby made it to the mid-point flag within seconds, and kept right on going. The shrill voices below became a chant— "Go! Go! Go!"—as he climbed higher and higher.

Not until he neared the top could Kate detect even the

slightest slackening of Toby's steady, rope-eating pace. When he reached the iron bar, a piercing cheer welled up from below. Toby waved, then began working his way back down.

"How'd he do?" Mark called to Gavin.

Gavin tapped his watch. "Nineteen seconds flat."

Mark whistled, impressed. While Toby progressed down the rope, the hydrologist watched Lana, who had cheered the senior counselor along with the kids. For a moment, Kate felt sorry for Mark. He was trying so hard to impress Lana, but he couldn't possibly beat Toby.

Toby let go of the rope and dropped the final six feet into the sandpit, pegging his landing like a gymnast. The kids made a rush for him, and it took both Kate and Lana to get them cleared back out of the pit.

A flotilla of puffy white clouds drifted overhead. Kate noticed them as she absently returned to the tree where she had been standing, and half wished for another rainstorm that would save Mark from the humiliation of losing in front of Lana.

But Mark already had hold of the rope. He beamed confidently at Lana, whose hand went to the chain at her neck. Then he turned to Gavin . . . and winked.

"And . . . he's . . . off," Kate heard Gavin murmur under his breath as if he were calling a horse race.

Mark seemed to catapult off the ground. While Toby had raced up the rope, Mark appeared to sprint. His hands flew along the rope so fast that as far as Kate could tell, there was hardly any rhythm to it. She only had time to think that Mark's swift ascent reminded her of a carnival game where you tried to ring a bell by swinging a mallet that sent a metal weight shooting up a pole—and he was there.

After slapping the iron rod to which the rope was attached, Mark swept his arm wide like a circus performer. Kate wondered if she was the only person on the ground who realized he was looking straight at Lana.

Below, every face was turned skyward in utter, gaping silence. Even Zach Forrest had stopped flipping rocks to watch.

Only Gavin peered studiously at his watch, and without fanfare announced, "Eleven point three seconds, folks."

That seemed to break the spell. A loud cheer shattered the silence, shot through by an ear-splitting whistle from Toby.

As Mark gave his newfound fans a jaunty salute from high above, Kate sagged back against the tree trunk, out of breath. She gasped, "I feel like I've just gone up that rope myself."

"I felt the same way the first time I saw Mark pull that," Gavin said.

"But how does he do it?"

"First off, he doesn't have nearly as much weight as Toby to haul up there. But he's also had a lot of practice. We've been rappelling down into vertical cave shafts all summer, and what goes down must come up."

Kate looked at Gavin. "You can climb that fast too?"

"Only if the bottom of the rope is on fire."

They both laughed—and laughing with Gavin came so naturally to Kate that for just that moment she forgot to remind herself that it was a mistake.

Mark started down. When he reached the sandpit, Toby was the first to clap him on the back and shake his hand. Then the kids crowded around, making him look like a grinning Pied Piper.

Only two hung back. Zach still pitched stones at trees all by his lonesome. And Lana remained at the edge of the sandpit, wide-eyed and pale. She clutched her limestone pendant with both hands as if it were a bouquet of red, red roses from Brad Pitt—with maybe a box of luscious Swiss chocolates from Leonardo DiCaprio thrown in for good measure. Her face could have graced the front of the most sentimental Valentine's Day greeting card.

Kate envied Lana for having lost her heart to a man who wanted her with all of his. She couldn't imagine a more perfect world than that.

Suddenly, being next to Gavin—close enough to touch with just the slightest movement of her arm—was too painful a place to be. Kate moved away quickly.

Standing alone well away from the sandpit, Zach looked about as lonely as Kate felt. She ached for the boy, understanding perfectly how it felt to be miserable amidst so much excitement. So instead of melting into the crowd gathering around Mark in the sandpit, she went to join the boy.

"What did you think of Toby and Mark?" she asked him. "Pretty slick climbing, huh?"

Zach shrugged as if he hadn't bothered to watch, but then said, "Mr. Harris lost."

"He doesn't seem upset by that. Mr. Eisly won fair and square."

"Mr. Harris lost all the same."

"Yes, but he believed in himself enough to try his best. Don't you think that's more important than who won or lost?"

Zach pitched more pebbles, giving no indication as to whether he agreed or disagreed.

"Look, Zach, each and every one of us here is a VIP— a Very Important Person. Because of that, the choices we make in our lives are important too. Sometimes those choices affect other people's lives too. So if we don't trust ourselves, if we don't have faith in ourselves, other people won't trust us or our choices."

The boy squinted at her, and Kate had a sense that she wasn't making any sense at all to him. In desperation, she pointed at Toby and gave it another try. "Okay, Mr. Harris didn't win this competition. But do you think the kids will no longer trust him as their counselor because of that?"

Zach shrugged again, and then shook his head.

"Why?" Kate asked, sensing a tiny connection and willing it to grow.

But he simply turned away and resumed pitching stones.

The sky had gone overcast again. It wasn't raining, but a fine mist began to fall. That dampened Kate's mood even more. Until that moment, she hadn't thought it possible for her spirits to sink any further as she stood there between the boy and the man who were both beyond her reach.

"I'm sorry, Zach," she said on impulse, smoothing the hair back from his forehead as she had so many times as he struggled through nightmares.

Zach reflexively ducked his head away, eyeing her curiously. "For what?"

"For letting you down this summer."

He looked bewildered.

Of course, she thought, Zach didn't understand that it was her job to get through to him, to help him find his way out of his emotional wilderness. So he didn't know that in not finding a means to do that, she had failed him, his mother, Cliff Peet, and herself.

All Zach understood was that he didn't want to be where he was, feeling the pain of loss that he did.

Kate sensed that she was being watched. She glanced back to where she had left Gavin, and found him studying her with a worried expression. She forced a smile that she didn't feel. And though he returned it, he still looked concerned.

Once the commotion over the impromptu climbing competition had abated, Toby turned the kids' attention back toward assembling the makeshift stretcher that they had abandoned. The boys stripped off their Camp Reliant T-shirts, and Annie Rich threaded the saplings through the T-shirts' bottoms and armholes.

Then they took a vote on who would get to ride back to camp on the contraption while the rest took turns carrying. Lightweight Tommy Reyes got elected to ride, for once gaining a privilege based on his small size. Zach was named to the lead-off team of stretcher-bearers, a task that he accepted less grudgingly than Kate had expected.

Before Zach hefted his share of the load, he gave Tommy a swat on the shoulder. Tommy looked up at him and grinned. To Kate's surprise, the two exchanged a high-five.

"Will wonders never cease?" a voice whispered near Kate's ear. Toby had moved to her side, holding the first-aid manuals belonging to the stretcher-bearers.

She nodded. "Who would have expected Zach and Tommy to become best buds?"

"I was referring to Lana and Mark. Don't look, but they're all but holding hands."

Kate did look. She couldn't resist. Sure enough, the two were heading up the trail side by side, leading the procession back toward the camp compound.

Gavin had been right about one thing: Lana had indeed apparently forgotten all about being a good two inches taller than Mark.

"Listen, Kate," Toby said, "they're taking the point. I'll keep tabs on the stretcher crew if you and Gavin want to bring up the rear again."

Gavin was still standing by the tree. Kate glanced his way without making eye contact.

"That's all right, Toby." She sighed. "I'll monitor the stretcher." And she did, alone, through a succession of stretcher-bearer teams, all the way back to the compound.

An hour after returning to camp, Kate was sitting on the front porch of the main cabin, filling out individual performance sheets on the kids. Mark had insisted on helping Lana handle the lunch scene in the dining hall, so Kate was taking the opportunity to catch up on paperwork.

Gavin and Toby had joined Mickie Bonner in Cliff Peet's office. They had invited Kate along, but she had begged off. If they were hatching some grand plan for a new caving program for Camp Reliant, that was great. But she didn't think she, an as-yet unproven counselor, deserved a role in that decision-making.

She had made it halfway through the stack of papers when Mark Eisly emerged from the dining hall. Fists planted on his hips, he glanced around the clearing as though looking for someone. Spotting Kate sitting on the porch, he came striding over.

"I haven't congratulated you, Mark," she said. "You must be the world's fastest rope climber."

He gave her a friendly wink. "Second fastest."

"But you won. You beat Toby."

"I meant second next to Gavin. He taught me his technique, but I've never been able to beat him. Not that I haven't tried."

You should have tried today, Kate wanted to tell him. *You were out to impress the woman you love. That might have given you the edge you needed.* But saying right out loud that Gavin's attraction to her had its limits would have been too painful.

So Kate made herself change the subject. "Don't tell me you've had too much of the kids already."

"No way!" Mark glanced over his shoulder at the dining hall. "They're a terrific bunch. I come from a big family, so being around a horde of kids like that brings back a ton of fond memories. Makes me think I should become a science teacher." He rubbed his chin, as if that tongue-in-cheek idea just might have real merit. "Maybe that would win me more points with Lana. I'm going to marry that girl, you know."

"You're what?"

Mark laughed at her expression. "I know it sounds crazy, but love at first sight is sort of an Eisly family tradition. My dad fell for Mom the day they met back in high school. They got hitched right after college, and celebrated their thirty-fourth anniversary last month."

Kate recovered enough to ask, "Does Lana know about your plan?"

"Nope. Don't want to hit her with too much all at once, and scare her off."

"Good idea."

Mark's confession had left Kate a little out of breath. Gavin had mentioned that his friend was taken with Lana, but she'd had no idea that Mark already had marriage in mind. The contrast between Mark's ready willingness to commit, and Gavin's reluctance to even consider that risk, couldn't have been greater.

He scanned the clearing again. "Say, Lana sent me to find out if anyone's seen a kid named Zach Forrest."

Kate straightened. "Zach is missing?"

"Well, he wasn't when we all got back to camp. But he must have slipped away during lunch."

Suddenly uneasy, Kate indicated the cabin directly across the clearing from the dining hall. "Maybe he went back to the boys' dorm." She started to get up, but Mark motioned for her to stay put.

"You're probably right," he said. "I'll check it out."

As Kate watched Mark amble across the clearing, the performance sheets lay ignored on her lap, that uneasy feeling lingering like an echo of something larger. She had about decided to get up and follow Mark, when the screen door to her right swung open.

She glanced up at Gavin.

He quietly eased the screen door shut, a serious expression furrowing his brow.

"How's it going in there?" Kate asked, her uneasiness about Zach now overlain with an edgy nervousness. When Gavin looked at her, she felt transparent, as if he could peer right into her and read her recent ponderings about him.

"Okay, I guess," he said. "Mickie has convinced your boss that a caving program for Camp Reliant would be a knockout idea. But as the saying goes, the devil is in the details. They're both too stubborn for their own good, so negotiations are going to follow a winding, rocky road. I left Toby in there as referee."

Her gaze shifted back across the clearing to where Mark was just climbing the steps to the boys' dorm. Right then, she reminded herself, Zach was more important than whatever was or was not going on between her and Gavin Buckley.

Gavin came over and leaned against the porch railing directly in front of her, blocking her view. She was forced to look at him, but found it difficult to meet his intense gaze.

"Kate, what's wrong?"

"Oh, probably nothing." She tried to look around him. "Zach Forrest is temporarily unaccounted for."

He leaned forward and cupped her chin in one hand, forcing her to look at him. "I'm not talking about Zach. I'm talking about us. Ever since I got here today, you've been trying to steer clear of me. Right now, you won't even look me in the eye."

She did meet his gaze then, a glancing blow that caused a flutter in the general vicinity of her heart. Gavin released her chin but didn't draw back.

"Talk to me, Kate." His voice softened. "Last night under the stars, I thought . . ." He rubbed his hands together, his lips a tense line. "I thought we made some kind of connection."

Kate swallowed, making a small clicking sound in her throat. Her gaze lowered to his lips—so taut with concern now, but so tender and warm last night. The flutter in her chest became an ache.

"Gavin, I care about you very much," she said in the understatement of the century. "Too much to be your friend."

His mouth opened, and then closed. Opened again.

For a moment, he looked so comically nonplused that Kate would have laughed if she hadn't been afraid she would cry instead. She did manage a tentative smile, and that made her just brave enough to be honest. Yes, Kate decided, honesty would be the best policy. Better to suffer the pain now than later, when it would only be a whole lot worse.

"Gavin, I like you very much," she repeated, then took a deep breath and let out the rest. "I also happen to be falling in love with you."

His eyes lit up, the pupils dilating. His expression relaxed into a gentle smile of pure pleasure. He reached for her hands, but she quickly tucked them beneath the papers in her lap.

"Let me finish," she said, hurrying on before her nerve gave out. "To put it as simply as possible, loving you is a dead-end road that I cannot afford to take."

He looked startled for a few seconds, and then backed off, his expression shuttering. "Interesting," he said evenly. "I've never been called a dead-end road before."

"Not *you*, Gavin! I just meant—"

He held up a hand, cutting her off. "All I want to know—" He paused, lowering his voice, seemingly straining to maintain calm. "—*all* I want to know is why you think loving me is such a problem for you."

Keep it simple, Kate thought. Her hands trembled, causing the papers to rattle. She covered the sound by clearing her throat. *Keep it simple.*

"I love you, Gavin," she said, relieved that the tremor in her hands hadn't transmitted itself to her vocal cords. "But to my mind, love means commitment."

"And?" he said, warily.

"And . . . and if I let myself love you with all my heart, I'll just end up losing you. You've already made quite clear how much you doubt the concept of marriage. Your tolerance for taking risks, it seems, has its limitations." Her voice tried to crack just a little, but Kate was determined to get out the rest. "And if I'm around you, Gavin, I'll want to risk everything. I *will* love you heart and soul—I won't be able to help myself."

"Katie . . ." He stared at her. Rubbed his face hard as if trying to clear his head. Stared at her some more.

His obvious agitation puzzled Kate. She had expected Gavin to feel relieved that she was letting him off the hook by not trying to force commitment on him. But he didn't look at all relieved. He looked like a man who had just discovered that his wallet was missing.

By this time, Kate was feeling pretty darned agitated herself. But before either of them could bring their difficult conversation to a merciful close, she caught movement from the corner of her eye and glanced past Gavin toward the boys' dorm.

Mark had just emerged from the dorm. He stood on the top step for a moment, rubbing his chin, then came on across the clearing toward the main cabin. Something about his frown and the way he picked up his pace the closer he came alarmed Kate.

She was on her feet by the time he reached the porch.

Mark bounded up the steps and planted his fists on his hips, casting a troubled glance back at the boys' cabin.

"What is it?" Kate asked. Anxiety whisked through her like an icy-hot wind.

"I'm not entirely sure, Kate," he said. "But I think we might have a serious problem."

Chapter Eight

A damp, gusty wind whipped leaf litter across the trail. To the north, a shelf of blue-black clouds shouldered over the mountain. But the weather was the farthest thing from the minds of the three adults gathered just below the entrance to the cave.

Securely chained and padlocked, the steel gate that secured the entrance against trespassers was unchanged.

The mountainside around it was not.

Kate was stunned by the devastation that nature had wrought since she had been there last. Above and to the left of the entrance, rains had loosed a slide of mud and rock twenty feet wide, uprooting the big lightning-blasted hickory tree that had stood next to one of the gate's posts. The shift in the terrain had left a narrow space between the top of the post and the mountainside.

"Do you think Zach could squeeze through that opening?" she asked.

"Like soap through a wet fist," Gavin said, and went clambering up the loose rubble of the slide.

Kate gave chase. Thanks to her lighter weight, she was

able to overtake and pass him. Mark followed. At the gate, Gavin rattled the bars and jerked the padlock.

"Do you have a key to this thing?" he asked Kate. "Mine's back in the Hummer."

"Mr. Peet's is hung up in his office," she said.

"Could be Zach isn't in there," said Mark.

"I hope he isn't," Kate said. "But you heard Tommy. Zach's been plotting to get back into the caves ever since we put up the gate."

"Yeah." Mark hissed in exasperation, shaking his head. "And there were those homemade charts he'd drawn, all lain out on his bunk."

They both turned to Gavin.

He peered through the gate into the cave, then up at the narrow gap near the post. "I know one thing," he said at last. "If I were the kid, I'd sure as blazes be in there if I'd been given this much of a chance."

Kate groaned, though Gavin had only told her what she had already feared. "We have to find out for sure."

Mark popped them both on the shoulder. "Sit tight. I'll hightail it back to camp and get the key. Be back here in a jiff."

"You'd better alert Mr. Peet," Kate said, grateful to Gavin for remaining with her. She wouldn't have left the cave entrance under any circumstances.

"And bring as much gear as you can carry," Gavin called after Mark, who was already sprinting down the trail.

When they were alone, Kate pressed her face to the gate bars. "Maybe Mark is right. Maybe Zach isn't in there."

"Wishful thinking."

Kate cupped her hands beside her mouth and shouted Zach's name at the top of her lungs. The sound echoed against limestone, mocking her. They held their breath for a moment, listening to the silence. Then Gavin jerked at the chain again, his impatience growing.

"Well, I can't just wait around like this," she said, having stood it as long as she could. "I have to know for sure."

Kate scrambled up the rock fall to the top of the gate-post and thrust both legs through the opening. Her hips stuck. Gavin reached through the bars and grabbed the soles of her sneakers, supporting part of her weight. With some of the pressure off her hips, she gave a wriggle and popped on through to her waist.

"Okay," he said, "now turn slightly to your left, and tilt your shoulders."

Kate did as instructed. A shower of dirt and pebbles accompanied her short fall. She hit the ground off-balance, landing as inelegantly as a load of muddy laundry. But she was on the other side of the gate.

She got up, brushed herself off, and looked through the bars at Gavin. "Trust me. You'd never fit."

He bared his teeth and rattled the bars one more time, like a desperately frustrated convict. Only he wanted in, not out.

Looming clouds outside had shortened the twilight zone within the cave entrance. Kate could see no more than a few yards into the passage. She almost didn't notice the nylon bag crumpled on the shadowed floor.

She went over and picked it up. A sickening fist clenched in her stomach as she read the name stenciled on the webbed shoulder-strap. "Gavin, this is Zach's. And it's empty."

He grimaced. "That boy . . ."

"Don't say it. Just . . . don't . . . say it." Already overwrought, she couldn't bear to hear Gavin's apprehension expressed in words.

Zach well might be in danger at that very moment, lost in the complex cave system. Kate knew she was being irrational, that his being there wasn't really her fault, but in her present state of mind, she was close to being eaten alive with guilt.

She took a step back. Her foot came down on a loose rock, and both legs went out from under her. As she picked herself up, muttering, her hand touched a cone-shaped object. Kate picked it up, realizing as she did so that she hadn't tripped on a rock after all.

She turned the cone of waxed packaging twine over in her hands, trying to figure out what it was doing there. Dozens of such cones were stocked back at Camp Reliant, the twine used for everything from emergency shoelaces to tying rolled mattresses on unused bunks.

Then she figured it out.

Kate knelt near the gate, peering intently at the ground. The twine was almost the same color as the dirt, so it took her a minute or two to spot what she was looking for.

There it was—an end of twine attached to the bottom of one of the bars with a neat slipknot. Riding an eager wave of discovery, she picked up the twine and followed it deeper into the cave.

"Kate, where the devil are you going?"

"Just . . . in here."

With each step, Kate's excitement swelled. And with each step, she kept telling herself that she really did intend to go just a little ways farther, just to make sure.

"Kate! Come back here!"

"Okay. Just a sec," she called back, already far enough

along the passage that she had to raise her voice. "Be right back."

Behind her, the bars rattled loudly.

By the time Mark came jogging up the trail from Camp Reliant, lugging a heavy equipment bag from the Hummer, Gavin had nearly paced a rut into the ground in front of the locked gate. He ran down the slope to meet Mark.

"Where's the key?" he demanded, resisting the urge to grab Mark by the collar of his coveralls and shake the key out of him.

"Take it easy, Gav." Mark dropped the gear bag and rolled a kink out of his shoulder. Unzipping a pocket in his sleeve, he dug in with one finger and came out with a padlock key.

Gavin snatched it from him. He sprinted back up to the gate as Lana Peet and Mickie came hurrying up the trail, followed by Toby Harris. Gavin ignored all of them and concentrated on fitting the key into the padlock on the chain that secured the gate.

"Where's Kate?" Mark asked.

A few seconds later, the two women joined them and echoed Mark's question.

"She climbed down through that crevice." Gavin indicated the space above the gate post where Kate had dropped through. He'd tried to enlarge the opening after she slipped deeper into the cave, but had hit solid limestone.

"Well, I don't see her," Mark said, peering through the bars.

Gavin barked a humorless laugh. "Join the club." The padlock finally snapped open. He jerked the chain clear and threw the gate wide. "Get the gear, Mark. Step on it."

Mark raced back to the gear bag as Mickie gripped Gavin's arm and turned him around. "Did Kate go on into the cave?" she asked.

"She did. And blind as a bat, she was." Gavin winced as if he'd taken a blow. "Far as I know, she wasn't even carrying a match."

Mickie looked worried. "But she couldn't have gone far in the dark."

"You don't know Kate O'Riley. She's one determined woman where her kids are concerned." *Too determined for her own good,* he added to himself.

Mark dumped the gear bag at their feet. Gavin dropped to his knees and began pulling out his coveralls, and their hardhats, ropes, and other equipment.

"So you're sure the boy is in the cave too?" Mickie asked.

"He's in there." Gavin stepped back into the cave and changed quickly into his coveralls.

Toby Harris shoved through the gate, squinting into the half-light of the cave. When he spotted Gavin snapping up his coveralls, he held up a flashlight. "I brought a light. I'll go in with you."

Gavin took one look at the counselor's formidable size and said, "We'll be getting into some pretty tight places in there, Toby. You'll slow us down."

When Toby started to protest, Mickie stepped up and took him by the arm. "We'd better call county search-rescue just in case, don't you think, Gavin?"

"It wouldn't hurt. I'm betting we'll find Kate and Zach all right, but I wouldn't mind a little backup just in case I'm wrong."

"Then let's go," Mickie said to Toby. "We have work to do."

Toby balked briefly, then reluctantly turned and followed her down the slope.

When they were gone, Gavin strapped on a gear belt, then grabbed up a hardhat. He and Mark each shouldered a coil of nylon rope. They were lighting their carbide lanterns when the gate whined on its hinges.

Mark glanced toward the entrance. "Lana!"

She stood beside the gate, hugging herself, looking distressed. "Mark, I—" Her voice choked off.

"Hey, there." Mark set aside his hardhat and hurried to her. "What is it?"

"This is my fault," she said, close to tears. "I should have kept a sharper eye on Zach. But I didn't, and he took off and . . ."

"Now stop that. Zach is going to be just fine. Trust me."

A tear rolled down her cheek. "You're just trying to make me feel better."

Mark took her face in his hands. The ground sloped down in Lana's direction, so they were eye to eye. He gazed intently at her until he had her complete attention.

"Butterfly," he said firmly, "I'd do anything to make you feel better right now—anything but lie to you. Zach will be okay."

She hitched a breath, her effort to smile meeting with little success. "I'll wait right here."

Mark nodded. "Do that, Butterfly. We'll try not to keep you waiting long." He thumbed the tear from her cheek, gave her a quick peck on the nose, and turned away.

"Mark!"

He looked back at her as he donned his hardhat.

"Please," she said. "Be careful, Mark." She was clutching at the pendant he had given her, as if holding it tightly might keep him safe.

"Always," he said.

Mark exchanged a glance with Gavin, and whispered, "I've gone absolutely foolish over that girl, Gav. You'll be best man at our wedding."

Gavin hitched up his gear belt and led the way deeper into the cave's twilight zone. "Don't you think you'd better ask her first?"

"I will when the time's right. You can't rush these things. She's still pretty young, so Cliff Peet will probably want us to have a long engagement."

By the time they made their way into the dark reaches of the cave system, Mark had fallen silent—probably making a mental list of future wedding guests, Gavin figured. He felt a sharp twinge of envy for his friend.

The utter silence wasn't so bad. It was the waiting that began to get to Kate—waiting in darkness so complete that she wasn't always certain whether her eyelids were open or closed.

What bothered her more was the dank chill. Sitting against the craggy limestone wall, hugging her knees, she wished she had worn something warmer than shorts. At the moment, that old Penn State sweatshirt that Gavin had loaned her would have felt like a warm security blanket.

And of course, there was Zach. She hoped he had dressed warmly.

Kate wasn't sure how long she had been sitting there alone. Having accidentally dropped the waxed twine that Zach was feeding out as he explored the cave system, she could no longer continue following the boy. Neither could she backtrack to the cave's entrance without risk of becoming lost.

Gavin had been right about one thing—for anyone who was down in the maw of a cave without a light, all bets were off. And stupidly, Kate had neglected to bring so much as a candle.

So she sat. And waited.

Though she had called out to Zach so many times that her voice had grown hoarse, she hadn't heard so much as a peep from him. He had to be somewhere up ahead, probably still doling out yards and yards of twine to mark his return route. Unlike Kate, he probably wasn't lost at all. At least, she hoped not.

Kate didn't want to think about the possibility that Zach, too, had dropped the twine and couldn't find it. Surely the boy had at least brought a flashlight.

Suddenly, a sound.

She cocked her head, straining to hear. There, again. Her name echoed down the passageway, eerily spectral. Kate scrambled to her knees, giddy with relief. The sound hadn't come from all that far away.

Kate shouted back.

Gavin's voice came back to her with the speed of an echo, though she couldn't make out what he said. A moment later, a wavering glow appeared in the distance.

"You're getting closer," she cried.

The glow moved nearer and grew brighter until it split, taking the shape of two carbide lanterns. At last, Gavin appeared, moving quickly toward her, followed closely by Mark. The two men were hunkered over beneath the low ceiling, their equipment rattling on their belts. Lantern-glare prevented Kate from seeing their faces. Not until Gavin was five feet away did she realize he was fighting mad.

"Blast it, Kate, you couldn't have waited fifteen minutes?"

"It was dark," she said. "I couldn't see my watch."

Through his teeth he muttered, "This is not funny."

"So who's laughing?"

Gavin gave a snarl—an excellent imitation of a ferocious dog—and whipped off his hardhat with its open-flame carbide lantern. Before Kate knew what was happening, he walked right up and planted a kiss firmly on her lips.

"You can be an incredibly frustrating woman, Katie O'Riley," he said, folding her in his arms. "Confounding, frustrating . . ."

Kate's head was still reeling as Gavin released her, but she heard Mark's chuckle as plain as day. Mark was carrying a gear bag, and had a spare hardhat hooked to his belt. Gavin took the hardhat, lit the lantern, and clapped the hat onto Kate's head.

"Lana is waiting back at the entrance," Mark said. "Mickie took Toby back to camp to start coordinating. They'll have Mr. Peet contact the regional search-and-rescue people just in case, if he hasn't already. But I figure it'll take them at least a couple of hours to get experienced cavers organized and in here." He patted Kate's arm reassuringly. "If Zach is in this system, we'll find him."

"He's here," Kate said with absolute conviction.

Gavin's lantern illuminated her face as he turned toward her. "You've been following the twine from the gate, haven't you?"

"Yes. But I dropped it, and couldn't find it in the dark."

He bent with his hands clasping both knees, sweeping

his light slowly across the cave floor. Within seconds, he leaned down and picked up the twine.

"I've come upon one knot so far," she said, taking the twine from him. "So Zach is at least on his second spool. But there's no telling how many spools he brought with him."

"It would help if we knew where the boy is headed." Gavin eased past Kate and peered deeper along the passage. "But since he surely can't have been this deep into the system before, he can't know where he's going himself."

"No, but he might know where he's trying to go," Mark said. "While I was back at the camp getting the gate key and raising the alarm, Tommy Reyes overheard us talking about Zach and got real upset. He says he and Zach had talked about the trip you two made down here—Tommy kept referring to the cave system as magical. He said Zach seemed pretty intrigued by that."

Kate closed her eyes briefly. She had used the term *magical* when describing her caving adventure to Tommy. Now she wondered if that word might have been a serious mistake.

"So I figure Zach is down here to see the sights, assuming he can find them on his own." Mark paused. "My guess is that he'll keep right on going until he sees something interesting. Or until he reaches the end of his twine, whichever comes first."

That got all three of them moving.

As they pressed forward, following the twine, they stopped frequently to call Zach's name. Each time they got no answer, the silence seemed to drive them along even faster. By the time they paused in a snug crawl space to drink from Gavin's water bottle, all of them were hoarse from shouting. Then they took turns squeezing through a narrow space that Kate didn't remember from her earlier exploration with Gavin.

"These passages remind me of an ant colony my sixth-grade science teacher kept on his desk," Kate said. She hadn't intended her remark as a joke, but it drew dry laughter from both men. The sound lifted her spirits a little.

All they had to do was follow the brown waxed twine, she told herself, and they were bound to catch up with Zach. They might even bump into him on his way back toward the entrance. Either way, she thought, surely their search wouldn't last much longer.

Then the twine ran out.

Kate gasped as the end of it slipped from her grasp. In the lead, Gavin stopped and looked back at her. She retrieved the end and held it up for all to see. A hiss of air escaped through both men's teeth—stereo chagrin.

"I cannot believe Zach went on after his twine ran out." Kate felt like weeping.

Gavin wrapped a hand firmly around hers. "He'll be all right, Kate."

"But without the twine, Zach could be anywhere in here. This is like hunting for a needle in a haystack."

"Not quite." Gavin's mud-streaked features creased into a frown. "Needles don't think."

"Oh." She didn't see how that made any difference. "Are you saying you can read Zach's mind?"

"No, Kate, but maybe you can. You know him a lot better than Mark or I do." He looked at her expectantly. "The boy wouldn't have come this far into the caves just out of curiosity. Come on . . . what do you think has caused him to be so obsessed with this place?"

Kate put some thought into that, though it wasn't easy at first in her current state of mind. What she knew for sure was that Zach was lonely, he still deeply missed his father, and the Camp Reliant experience hadn't worked out for him. The child wanted to go home, but according to his mother, he had been so out of control lately that even that might not be an option.

A knot formed in Kate's throat as she mentally ticked off items on what she had come to think of as Zach Forrest's list of despair. He didn't seem to have anything going for him that summer. And yet, she had seen him around Tommy Reyes. She knew in her own heart that Zach was—could be—a good and decent kid.

If only I could have reached him.

Life had led Zach down a rough patch of road, leaving him feeling lost, alone and—though he would never admit it—frightened. So what, Kate asked herself, would she be looking for if she were in the boy's shoes at that moment?

The light at the end of the tunnel.

That felt right, but somehow didn't make sense. You didn't venture deep inside a limestone mountain, alone, in search of light. Not unless . . .

Gavin had been watching Kate, waiting. When she finally looked at him, his expression brightened, becoming hopeful.

"I know," she said. "I *think* I know. Zach is down here in search of the magic."

"Say what?" Mark exchanged a blank look with Gavin.

"Tommy asked me what it was like down here," Kate explained. "I told him the cavern was magical—that's why he used that word when he talked to you about it." Maybe she had oversold that a bit. But she didn't think so. What could be more magical than cave pearls and moonmilk? "Anyway, Tommy obviously passed that along to Zach. And since Zach had already found this cave system, well, it must have seemed like a natural place to find some of that magic."

"Literally? Magic?"

"It sounds crazy to you because you're an adult," she said. "But Zach's just a kid . . . and a pretty desperate one at that."

Gavin was still holding her hand. When his grip tightened, Kate felt a powerful urge to throw herself into his arms. She needed the warmth of his embrace for just a moment, even if it wasn't forever. She needed reassurance that what she was saying made sense.

And the way Gavin looked at her fulfilled both of those needs. He gave Kate a crooked grin that seemed to pour right down into her, warming her from the inside out. Then he nodded, slowly, the way a person does when he sees difficult puzzle pieces slide neatly into place.

"I don't think for a second that Zach really and truly believes in magic," she added. "But—"

"But he's looking for a way out of himself," Gavin interrupted, still nodding.

"Not exactly. More like a way *back to* himself."

"Okay. Yeah. Like when I was a kid and got stuck in that crawl space. A magic awakening."

Mack shifted his weight, the wash of his lantern dancing as he glanced from one face to the other. "Beg your pardon folks, but you two have kinda lost me here."

Kate turned to Mark with an intensity that appeared to startle him. "Zach is testing himself, Mark. He's testing his power to believe in himself." She held up the end of the twine. "But he's let go of his safety line." Huge risk, there. "What if he's lost?"

"Then we'll find him," Gavin said firmly.

Mark nodded.

Gavin aimed his lantern ahead, and then flicked it to the left where a seam in the limestone took off at yet another right angle. They were well into the damp zone now. Moisture glistened on the walls and ceiling, and made footing treacherous at times when they could stand at all.

"Well," he said, "Zach could have gone either way here. Straight ahead, or left."

"This seam could be another dead-end," Mark said. "I'll check it out while you two keep going. If it's a dud, I'll catch up. That'll double our chances of running across the kid."

"Go." Gavin lightly slapped the side of Mark's helmet.

As soon as Mark vanished into the narrow side passage, Kate and Gavin continued on ahead.

Ten minutes later, Kate halted suddenly and picked up a length of red, blue, and yellow braided yarn about six or eight inches long. "Gavin!"

He was a little out front. He stopped and backed toward her.

She showed him her find. "It's a friendship bracelet. The kids were making and exchanging them the other day." Kate had seen Tommy braiding this very color combination, and was certain Zach was the only youngster he would have given it to.

"This is Zach's?" Gavin asked.

Kate wanted to laugh. "Who knows? This is such a popular place, anyone could have dropped it."

Gavin smiled at her sarcasm. "Guess I had that coming, didn't I? At least we know we're headed in the right direction."

He put a thumb and forefinger to his mouth and sent an incredibly penetrating whistle down the passage toward where they had parted ways with Mark. Seconds later, they heard a distant return whistle, repeated twice.

"We'd better wait for Mark to catch up," he said. "Don't want to get our troops spread unnecessarily thin."

Kate didn't want to wait. She wanted to forge ahead, and scratch the mental itch that kept telling her that Zach Forrest was just around the next turning, just beyond the next crawl space, just a little farther along. But of course, Gavin was right to wait for Mark. If a search party wasn't coordinated, they could end up wasting a lot of time searching for each other.

As if sensing Kate's distress, Gavin shifted suddenly and pulled her into his arms, automatically dodging the lantern on her hardhat.

"I'm sorry," she said. "I'm just so worried. I thought we'd have found Zach by now."

Gavin shushed her. She settled against him, aware for the first time that she was bone-tired. But she knew that most of that weariness was from sustained stress. If Zach crawled out of the darkness right then, sheer joy would wash away her fatigue in an instant.

"You have nothing to be sorry for," he said softly. "Nothing at all."

"Oh, but I do. If I'd been any good as a counselor, Zach wouldn't have broken the rules and come in here."

"If you'd been a bad counselor," Gavin countered, "you wouldn't have come after him."

Stress stung at the back of Kate's eyes. She closed her eyelids, fighting back the tears. *This isn't a time for falling apart,* she thought. *Stay focused on Zach.*

After a while, Gavin's hand moved gently to the back of her neck. "Kate O'Riley," he murmured, "I love you so blasted much."

Her eyes shot open. For a moment, Kate couldn't

breathe. Then she took a great gulp of air and disengaged herself from his embrace so she could look at him. And sure enough, there it was written all over his face—pure, honest, wide-awake love. Maybe she somehow should have seen that coming, but she hadn't. And something in Gavin's expression told her that he hadn't either.

Kate's pulse quickened with excitement. For just a moment, she dared to dream. But then she got a grip on herself, taking a firm hold on reality. With Gavin, she realized, that's all it ever would be . . . a dream. He might be able to love with all his being, but that didn't mean he would ever let go of his doubts about marriage.

In place of the shining dream, all Kate could see was the hopelessness of it.

"Why are you shaking your head?" he asked, reaching out to trace a fingertip along the curve of her cheek, then her jaw.

She seized his hand in both of hers so he would stop touching her that way. "You know why, Gavin. You know how you feel about . . . about marriage. You don't see it as a reasonable risk."

She tried to laugh, to make light of her pain, but it came out sounding like shattering glass. Kate forced out the words that she didn't want to hear, knowing how necessary it was to clear the air once and for all.

"We don't want the same things out of a relationship, Gavin. This needs to stop right now. If we let ourselves love each other, knowing there's no future in it, we'd both end up getting hurt—badly." *It's already too late for me to avoid that,* she thought, feeling a ragged gash widening in her heart. "We would end up being no better off than Zach, wandering around in the dark searching for a way out of the pain."

His cheeks twitched as if he, too, were already feeling the pain. "That's crazy, Kate."

She nodded. "I know it's crazy. But that doesn't make it any less true. You can wander around in the dark all you want, but that doesn't mean you'll ever find the magic. Not by yourself."

Kate raised his hand and pressed her lips to his palm. She felt drained. Delivering that necessary little speech was just about the hardest thing she had ever done.

With a sigh, she released his hand. Hearing Gavin Buckley say that he loved her was a treasure that she would carry with her for the rest of her life. She would keep that tucked away in the same drawer with her broken heart.

Chapter Nine

When Mark caught up, he found Kate and Gavin backed up against opposite walls of the passage. They were just sitting there with their feet inches apart, staring at each other as if separated by the Grand Canyon. They hardly registered his arrival.

Mark said, "What's up, folks?"

Kate blinked at him for a few seconds, then held up the braided friendship bracelet that she had found. "Zach has been this way."

"Whoa. It's a good thing you have evidence that he came this way. That seam that I took back there looked like it might keep going forever."

Kate rolled to her feet. This time, she took the lead before either Mark or Gavin could get ahead of her. She moved quickly, refocusing her mind as best she could. It was almost a relief to concentrate on Zach again—to look forward to finding the boy, instead of looking back at something that never could be.

A moment later, the ceiling lowered abruptly, forcing them to their hands and knees. Kate squirmed around a sharp bend, and suffered yet another disappointment at not encountering Zach. But she kept on going without pause now, ignoring her fatigue. Only Zach mattered now.

"Slow down, Kate," Gavin called from behind.

Mark added, "Watch for drop-offs."

The ceiling rose for a dozen or so feet along the passage, then again dipped so low that she had to duck-walk. Her hardhat banged sharply against an unseen knob of limestone overhead. Kate glanced up for a few awkward steps, scanning the ceiling for other hazardous outcroppings.

And suddenly the floor dropped out from under her.

Kate let out a shriek as she plummeted, arms and legs flailing. The scream and her fall came to a simultaneous end with a tremendous splash that extinguished her carbide lantern. She was plunged into total darkness in water cold enough to drive the air from her lungs.

Disoriented in the darkness, she half-drowned herself before realizing that the water was only waist-deep.

A light appeared high above. Kate just had time to shout, "Watch out for—"

And Gavin came tumbling down toward her. He swore out loud just before hitting the water flat on his back, sending a tidal wave into Kate's face. The water subsided, leaving her blinking and coughing. Gavin floated there for a moment, the wind knocked out of him.

After a lengthy pause, Kate finished saying, "—the drop-off."

At the sound of her voice, he turned his head toward her. The carbide lantern on his hardhat still burned brightly. When he saw that Kate was only waist-deep in water, he stood up.

Kate braced herself, expecting him to be angry with

her for having rashly grabbed the lead, and for leading them astray.

Instead, he took her by the shoulders, ever so gently, as though examining an object of exquisite fragility. "Are you okay?" he asked.

She nodded, shivering. The fall into the water pit had unnerved her. Gavin tucked her securely under his arm. She was grateful for his presence, at the same time wishing that she could have prevented his joining her there.

Together, they surveyed their surroundings—and their predicament—with the light from Gavin's lantern. They were in a deep, roundish hole roughly the size of Kate's room back at Camp Reliant. A shallow indoor swimming pool, she thought nonsensically.

"At least Zach isn't down here," Gavin said, sounding as relieved as Kate felt.

He turned and shone his light back up a precipitous incline—what looked like a ten-foot water slide with no handholds anywhere. Kate couldn't imagine how they were going to get themselves out of there.

Then Mark appeared at the top. When he saw that they were uninjured, he grinned. "How's the water down there, folks?"

"Eisly . . ." Gavin said, brittle warning in his tone.

Mark quickly backed out of sight. For a moment, Kate was afraid that Gavin had scared him away—but then a sound of metal being hammered into stone echoed down to the pit. Seconds later, a length of nylon rope sailed down to them.

Gavin took the rope without a word, and looped the end around Kate's waist.

"I'm sorry," she murmured. "This was really stupid of me."

"Keep in mind that I did a swan-dive too, Kate."

His voice sounded tight, and at first she thought Gavin had decided to be ticked off at her after all. But as he tugged the rope to make sure it was secure, she realized her error. He wasn't even close to anger. He had sounded . . . shaken.

"I'm okay," she told him again.

Gavin opened his mouth, but then his jaw snapped shut as though words were inadequate. Instead, he pulled her close and kissed her as if his life depended on it. Startled, Kate returned his kiss, barely aware that salty tears were streaming down her already wet cheeks.

She was still drifting in the safe harbor of Gavin's arms when they both became aware of a light shining down on them from above. They looked up to find Mark watching them from the top of the incline, his chin propped on one hand.

"Any old time y'all are ready," Mark said.

Gavin glowered up at him, an expression that most likely was lost in the glare of their lanterns. Then to Kate's astonishment, he bent and kissed her again right there in front of Mark before finally stepping aside.

"Well, if that doesn't beat all," Mark said, pretending to talk to himself. "I never would have taken that pit to be such a romantic situation. I guess it takes all kinds."

"Live it up while you still can, Eisly," Gavin said.

He and Kate waded over to the foot of the incline, where Kate took up the slack in the rope.

"Just keep the line untangled," he said. "Mark will pull you up."

"That won't be necessary," she said. "We have something similar to this on the camp's obstacle course."

Kate took a firm grip on the rope, leaned back in the water, and planted both feet on the steep incline. She paused only briefly to marshal her energy, and then began the slow trudge up the slide.

Gavin stood in water up to his hips, watching Kate take the last few steps up the incline. She was very good at that, he observed. There were times when he thought of her as being as delicate as crystal filigree. But in reality, she possessed amazing strength wrapped up in that deceptively small package.

And that was just the beginning of sweet Katie O'Riley. Gavin was just beginning to discover her endless complexities. She had profound strength that not even she was aware of, and at the same time was as ephemeral as moonlight. She was capable of loving deeply, but wouldn't allow herself to love blindly. She could walk right up a limestone wall, but still lacked total faith in herself.

Getting to know Kate was like discovering an uncharted continent. Gavin felt like Lewis and Clark . . . Marco Polo . . . Christopher Columbus.

He took a deep breath as she reached the top of the incline and Mark pulled her into the passageway out of sight.

As soon as she was safely out of the pit, Gavin leaned a hand against the damp limestone wall and lowered his head, enduring yet another wave of the soul-numbing shock that he had experienced earlier.

He couldn't remember ever feeling so alone—at least, not since he was a kid. And even that old abandonment was ancient history now, part of a different life. It had all come down to trust. He saw that plainly now. He had been betrayed as a child not much younger than Zach Forrest. After that, he had made up his mind not to let himself be vulnerable to that kind of pain ever again.

But then along came Katie O'Riley.

As he had tumbled over the drop-off into the pit, the single thought that seared through his mind had been that Katie had fallen too. And in the second or two that it had taken him to hit bottom—*splash* bottom was more like it—the flash-fear that he might have lost her had exceeded even his own basic animal terror of falling into the unknown. But he hadn't lost her. And when he'd finally gotten his feet under him and determined that Kate was alive and well, he had actually gone weak in the knees with relief.

Gavin bashed a fist against the limestone wall. "You are such an unbelievably thick-headed fool," he whispered.

Just days ago, he had been fool enough to tell Kate what he thought about marriage. At the time, he'd meant every word he had said. She had believed him then— and still believed him now.

But Gavin wasn't at all sure that he believed himself any longer.

The nylon rope sailed down from above and struck the top of his hardhat. Gavin grabbed hold and, without a thought of anything but Kate, climbed the slippery slope back up toward the woman he loved.

By the time Gavin made it back up to the passageway, Mark had changed and relit the carbide in Kate's lantern. While she and Gavin pulled off their hiking boots and wrung out their socks, Mark coiled the nylon rope and clipped it to his belt.

Kate had sat down a good five feet from Gavin and was trying her level best not to look at him. She felt emotionally whiplashed. On one side, she knew she couldn't let herself fall deeper in love with a man who apparently didn't think she was worth the risk of long-term commitment. But on the other side, she had come to realize that love had a will of its own. Between those two extremes, she felt as if she were being torn in half.

"We must have made a wrong turn," Kate said, concentrating on their objective as she relaced her boots. "Obviously, Zach didn't come this way."

Gavin seemed to have tended to his boots and socks entirely by touch. Ever since settling down in the passageway, he'd been staring straight ahead at the wall across from where he sat.

"I wouldn't be so sure," he said finally. Rolling onto his knees, he leaned his head close to the passageway floor and peered into the dark shadow beneath a jutting slab of limestone. He remained like that for several minutes, then said, "Well, well, well."

Mark got down on all fours and checked it out. "Oh, yeah," he said. "Definitely a home run."

Without looking up, both men motioned for Kate to join them.

She stretched out prone alongside Gavin and looked beneath the slab. Together, their three lanterns brightly illuminated a wide crawlspace about two feet high. The space extended beneath the slab for five or six feet, then seemed to expand into a larger area of indiscernible dimensions.

"Okay, ditch your lights," Gavin said.

They accomplished this by simply turning their hard-hats around like rally caps. The crawlspace went pitch dark.

He reached over and took Kate's hand. "Now watch."

She saw only darkness. "Gav . . ."

"Wait. Just watch."

So she waited. And she watched, with Gavin gripping

her hand as if he would never let go. One minute. Five minutes. Her hand grew warm in his. As the warmth grew, so did the rift in Kate's heart. And stuck smack in the middle of that rift was the nagging fear that they had been looking for what seemed like a long time, but hadn't found Zach.

She had failed to reach the boy. Now would she fail to find him?

Then, at long last, Kate saw the light.

Gavin took the lead in wriggling through the crawl-space, though he first had to carry on a brief but spirited argument with Kate over that privilege. He dropped out of sight on the far side, and for a moment she feared that he had fallen into another deep hole. But then he bobbed back into view, grinning fiercely.

He motioned Kate toward him. She shimmied on through, her pulse suddenly racing with anticipation. Kate had no idea what Gavin had found, other than the transient beam of light that they had spotted minutes earlier. But if the gleam in his eyes were any indication, she figured it had to be good news.

She could hear Mark following close behind her, bumping his gear bag ahead of him as he slithered along. She reached Gavin and he helped her out of the crevice, briefly blocking her view. But as he moved aside to give Mark a hand, she made a slow sweep with her lantern—and gasped.

Kate took two steps forward, but then found that she could make herself move no farther. For the first time in her life, she wondered if her eyes might be playing tricks on her. Was she really, truly seeing what she thought she was seeing?

Mark appeared at her side and let out a long, low

whistle. Then he couldn't seem to find words to go with that.

"Right." Kate came up with the only analogy that seemed to fit. "It's as big as a football stadium."

Gavin slid an arm around her. She felt his side shake with silent laughter. Without thinking, she put her arm around his waist.

"Maybe so," he said. "But I can't see a Green Bay Packer fitting through that crawlspace we just traversed."

The stunning size of the cavernous chamber was only the beginning. They swept their lights back and forth across its vast space, illuminating an army of strangely shaped stalagmites of varying heights. Massive stalactites hung from a ceiling as distant and dark as a midnight sky. Here and there, delicate formations protruded from the cavern walls like bizarre alien flowers. Every surface their lights touched glittered as if sprinkled with ice crystals.

Kate could only stare. The cavern that Gavin had shown her earlier in the week had dazzled her. The silent majesty of this one filled her with profound awe. The chamber might be as enormous as a football stadium, she thought, but it had the look of an enchanted castle.

Minutes drifted by, marked only by the slow, inexorable dripping of water onto limestone that had been going on for millions and millions of years. Time seemed to slow to a near-standstill, measured in eons instead of hours. Even the air felt ancient, as if they were breathing in the ages.

"To think," Kate said at last, "we're the first human beings to breathe this air."

"To be exact," said Gavin, "we're the second, third, and fourth."

She was still so dazed by the cavern that what he

meant took several seconds to register on her. When it did, she felt electrified. "Zach—"

"Take it easy. The boy is way over there." He pointed a little to the left, past a gargantuan calcite column. "I saw his flashlight again just before you made it through the crawlspace. The light looked pretty weak, but he seems to be moving around pretty actively. My guess is he's having a good look at the place."

"I can't believe he's really here," she said. *"Here."*

Kate was shaking so hard with excitement that she stumbled as she began to strike out across the wildly uneven floor of the cavern.

Gavin caught her, holding on until he was sure she had her footing back. "Take your time, Kate—watch where you put your feet. We don't need any sprained ankles here."

She remembered saying almost the same words to Tommy Reyes only yesterday. That seemed like a thousand years ago.

Kate paused long enough to shout, "Zach!" But she was so hoarse from calling out to the boy earlier that the name came out as a dry rasp.

She looked back at Gavin. He nodded, and loosed another piercing whistle that reverberated eerily off the cavern walls and formations, coming back to them from many directions.

The sound had not yet died away when Zach's familiar young voice called out, "Who are you?" He sounded curious, and perhaps a little wary—but not, as Kate had expected, frightened.

"Friends," Gavin called back, though his voice wasn't in much better condition than Kate's. "Stay put. We'll come to you."

"I can't," Zach returned. "I don't have time."

Worried that Zach might be moving away from them, and wondering why he didn't have time, Kate quickened her pace. She felt oddly as if she were picking her way through an ancient city of stunning architecture. Julius Caesar's Rome, or the Athens of Socrates. And yet, the bizarre calcite formations created a glittering fantasy world fit for goblins and fairies. She would not have believed that Zach Forrest could have made it all the way down there on his own—that he had been the first person to set foot in the vast natural chamber—if she hadn't followed him there herself.

Ahead lay a huge mound of what appeared to be a toppled column. Mark took the lead. He climbed until he found secure footing, then turned and helped first Gavin, then Kate to ascend past him. They kept leap-frogging each other, progressing a few feet at a time, until they reached the top.

There, Kate found Zach Forrest seated on a throne-like calcite formation, calmly changing the batteries in his flashlight. He grinned broadly at her and said, "Isn't this just the most awesome place you've ever seen?"

With a cry of relief, Kate closed the distance between them in a rush and scooped the boy into her arms. He gave a startled yelp as flashlight batteries scattered at their feet. She knew she was hugging him far too tightly, squeezing the very breath out of him. But she couldn't seem to make herself lighten up, not until she felt him patting her gently on the back.

"Oh, Zach, I'm so relieved that we've found you!" She held him at arm's length, inspecting for injuries. She couldn't find so much as a scratch.

"Found me?" Zach cocked his head and frowned, as if he might be just a shade worried about Kate. "But Miss O'Riley, I'm not lost."

Behind Kate, both men snorted.

Zach looked offended. "Well, I'm not. I strung two spools of twine from the entrance."

"The twine gave out a ways back, son," Gavin pointed out.

"Uh-huh." Zach nodded. "And I know just where it left off."

Clearly annoyed now, Zach picked up the scattered batteries, sat back down, and resumed inserting them into his flashlight. Kate sank onto her heels in front of him, not understanding why the boy didn't seem as relieved to see them as they were to find him.

Over his shorts he wore a waterproof canvas poncho. From clips on his belt hung a half-full water bottle, a clear plastic box containing two or three cookies, and—Kate blinked—another full spool of twine. Kate stared at that unused twine in disbelief.

As Gavin knelt beside her, Kate was distantly aware that Mark had wandered away to explore the mammoth chamber.

"Zach," she said, "Why didn't you tie onto the end of the last spool of twine?"

He snapped the batteries into place and switched on his flashlight—stalling, Kate thought. Apparently judging that the light wasn't necessary in addition to their carbide lanterns, he switched it off.

At last, he looked at Kate somewhat defiantly and said, "You'd just think I was stupid, Miss O'Riley."

Kate touched his cheek. "Zach, you can be very foolhardy at times. Coming down here was a dangerous thing to do, as you know. You don't like to follow rules, even when they're for your own good. You're quite capable of causing endless aggravation to a lot of people who want nothing more than to help you. But if there is one thing that you definitely are not, it's stupid."

She had no idea what Cliff Peet would think of that statement. But whether or not it was good counseling, it came straight from her heart. Zach Forrest was, in fact, one of the smartest youngsters she had ever met, though he generally took great pains to hide that fact.

Zach sucked in his lower lip. For the first time, he looked sheepish—and unexpectedly embarrassed. He lowered his chin and glanced at Kate and Gavin from under his dark brows.

"Well, you see . . ." He paused, seeming to search for more than just the right words. ". . . the twine was like . . ."

When Zach didn't finish the sentence, Gavin offered, "Like insurance?"

"Yeah!" Zach looked expectantly at Gavin, as if hoping the man might go ahead and explain the rest for him. Instead, Gavin simply draped an arm around Kate and waited. Zach's shoulders sagged.

"So what made you decide you didn't need the insurance anymore?" Kate asked.

Zach squirmed. Clearly, explaining himself wasn't something he enjoyed. Perhaps, Kate speculated, he had never gone so far as to think out his motivation.

"I had to find out," he said finally.

She inched closer. "Find out what?" They spoke in quiet tones, but even so their voices seemed loud in the yawning silence of the cavern.

"Find out if I could depend on myself." He bounced the flashlight against his bony knee. "It's like you said this morning, Miss O'Riley. If a person can't trust himself, how can anyone else trust him?" He sighed. "Even Tommy Reyes."

Kate was astounded to learn that her comments had played such a pivotal role in triggering Zach's trespass deep into the uncharted heart of the mountain. After more than five weeks of trying every way she knew to get through to the boy, she had finally succeeded, but with disturbing results.

"But Zach, what made you think letting go of the twine was a wise choice?"

"Oh, that's easy. I have a really good memory. You see, that's something I trust a whole lot. I made just two turns since the end of the twine, a right and a left. So when I leave here, I'll need to make first a right, then a left."

Kate and Gavin exchanged a glance.

"It was scary at first," Zach continued, "but I was careful not to go very far from the end of the twine. That's why I figured I didn't have time to wait for you to come to me a minute ago, when you hollered for me to stay where I was. I couldn't hang around wasting my flashlight batteries." Zach lifted his poncho to reveal a bulging cargo pocket in his shorts. "I brought a gob of spare batteries. When half of them ran out, I headed back."

"But Zach," Kate said, "what about the danger?"

He shrugged. "I was careful."

Gavin cleared his throat, drawing the boy's attention. "We had these, son," he said, tapping his carbide lantern.

"Yeah." Zach squinted into the light. "Way cool."

"And Mr. Eisly and I are experienced cavers."

"Yes, sir."

"Even so, have you noticed how wet Miss O'Riley and I are?" Gavin plucked at his still-soppy shirt.

Zach eyed their soaked attire curiously.

"We made a mistake and ended up falling into a deep

waterhole, Zach. A hole that we couldn't climb out of. No handholds, no footholds. Just belt-deep water."

"Wow." Zach looked back and forth at them. "How did you get out?"

Gavin nodded toward Mark, who was prowling around a good thirty or forty yards away. "Our friend threw us a rope. That's why it's important to *never* go caving alone, even if you're an expert."

"Gosh. If it wasn't for Mr. Eisly, you'd never have gotten out?"

"We'd have had one other good chance." Gavin held up a finger. "Before I came in here, I told people out on the surface where we were going. So if we don't return to the surface in a reasonable amount of time, they'll come searching for us."

Zach nodded. "Good idea."

"So," Kate put in. "Who did you tell that you were coming down here, Zach?"

The boy's ears reddened. "No one."

Kate took Gavin's hand, grateful to him, not just for helping to find Zach, but for getting involved in setting the boy straight instead of simply bawling him out. Not for the first time, she thought that Gavin Buckley might make a pretty fair youth counselor himself if he ever cared to take that up.

"Miss O'Riley?" Zach cast a hang-dog look at her. "I guess I'm in a mess of trouble, aren't I?"

"You violated a Camp Reliant rule by trespassing in this cave system," she said evenly, aware that this was the first time Zach had ever shown concern about being in Dutch over his behavior. "It's up to Mr. Peet to decide what to do about that."

"Oh." He made a worried face. "Will he boot me out of camp before Saturday's graduation?"

"I don't know, Zach. I'm sorry, but I just don't know."

"Oh, man," he said miserably. "What's Tommy going to think if I get sent home? And Mom—she'll have a fit."

"I don't think so," Kate said, ignoring Gavin's chuckle. "I think your mom will be glad that you're safe. She loves you very much."

"But she sent me to Camp Reliant. I didn't want to come."

"Do you think you gave her a choice?"

The sheepish look again. "I guess not."

Kate leaned over and gave the boy a hug. To her continued surprise, he hugged her back. She smiled, stroking the back of his head as her gaze drifted around at the incredible formations surrounding them.

Mark came clambering up the calcite heap toward them, as agile as a mountain goat. He said, "Mickie is going to do a double backflip when she finds out about this chamber. It's like nothing I've ever seen before."

Zach brightened. "Yeah, isn't it a blast? It's—" He glanced at Kate. "—it's magical. There's a place back over there that looks just like a forest of tree trunks."

"I saw it." Mark winked at Zach. "A magic forest."

All four of them stood and surveyed the cathedral-like grandeur of the huge cavern, their lantern light dancing over glittering spires and chandeliers of calcite. Yes, indeed, Kate thought, the magic of the place was one thing they all could agree upon. And as vast as the dazzling room already was, it continued to grow, to change, like life itself, although at a pace so slow as to be timeless.

Gavin slid his arm around her. "I told you coming down here would change your life," he said.

Kate reached up and took his hand—not, she realized, the hand that she had been holding a moment ago. This one was swollen. Upon closer inspection, she discovered the beginnings of a bruise along the outside edge.

He gently disengaged his hand from hers. When she gave him a quizzical look, he simply shrugged, a favorite gesture of Zach's that seemed to be contagious. Was she just imagining things, or did Gavin seem embarrassed by the swollen hand?

"We'd better get going," he announced before Kate could prod him for an explanation. "People outside are waiting for us."

They crept down off the mound and made their way back to the crevice that connected the cavern to the passageway. Mark entered the crawlspace first, followed by Zach. Before Kate could take her turn, Gavin embraced her once more, tightly.

"Kate," he whispered, "when I was falling into that pit, knowing you had fallen ahead of me . . ." He shook his head. "I've never been so terrified for anyone in my—"

"Hey, folks!" Mark called from the passageway. "Can we move it along in there?"

Gavin reluctantly released Kate and, one after the other, they traversed the crawlspace. On the other side, Zach was holding his flashlight under his chin, making spooky sounds. Normal kid stuff, Kate thought, and laughed along with Mark.

"Let's move on," Gavin said, unamused.

"Lighten up, Gav," Mark said, turning back toward the entrance.

But Kate had heard something in Gavin's voice that Mark must have missed. Back in the cavern, Gavin had sounded seriously disturbed while just talking about their fall into the waterhole. Now that they were all safely on their way out of the cave system, he seemed preoccupied and troubled . . . and *distant*.

Kate was acutely aware of Gavin's shifting mood, but too much had transpired in the past hours to dampen her spirits. Zach was finally making it through his dark period in more ways than one, and was on his way back to the light. With the boy in front of her and Gavin close behind, Kate had never felt so good—so *alive*—in her life.

The trek back to the cave entrance seemed to take forever. Gavin tried to keep everyone moving along at a steady pace, but that wasn't easy. Now that the Forrest kid had finally loosened up, he had turned into a regular chatterbox—one that couldn't seem to walk and talk at the same time.

Not that Kate and Mark were any help. Both kept plying the kid with endless questions about his solo journey into the cave, and were quite content to hang around listening to his lengthy responses.

Gavin had to give Zach credit for being a quick study. The boy had taken to heart their discussion of the wisdom of employing a buddy system when exploring. On the way out, Zach asked probing questions of his own about the cave system, and had repeatedly mentioned wanting to return with an expert. Gavin had a feeling that Zach was already thoroughly hooked on spelunking. And who could blame him, after today? As far as Gavin knew, no other twelve-year-old could boast of having discovered a cavern half as spectacular as the one they had just left.

Who are you kidding, Buckley? You never found one like that.

After a brief rest-break, they filed down a steep incline. Gavin took Kate's hand to help her maintain balance. She kept trying to look at his other hand, the swollen one that was beginning to hurt like blue blazes, but he kept it out of sight. He had already been enough of a fool without having to explain to her that he'd hauled off and belted a rock wall.

Maybe he should have banged his head against the wall instead, he thought. From the moment he had dropped over the edge into that water pit, he hadn't been able to shake the sense that he had already let something more priceless than gold dust slip through his fingers.

At the bottom of the incline, Gavin found that he didn't want to let go of Kate. Holding onto her had come to seem like the most important thing in his life. She had seemed so happy as they left the great cavern. But the closer they got to the entrance, the more he could sense her drawing away from him.

Just telling Kate that he loved her hadn't been enough. He should have known that it wouldn't, not when it came to someone as special as Kate O'Riley. Uttering that phrase had felt like such a bold, devil-may-care step to Gavin. Maybe it shouldn't have been. Maybe the sheer honesty of those words should have made them seem as easy and risk-free as taking his next breath.

Before meeting Kate, love hadn't meant much to him. Now it meant everything, but he might have already blown it. He had hurt Kate with his stubborn need to keep commitment at arm's length. As they neared the end of their journey through the mountain, she seemed to be trying to both literally and figuratively put him behind her.

At first, he couldn't believe how much that tore at him. Then a greater pain settled over him with all the darkness of a moonless night. Gavin grimaced, feeling like a man who had awakened too late to the realization that the one thing that he held most dearly was heading out the door without him. It was just like when he was a kid and his parents abandoned him and Mickie. Only then, it hadn't been his fault.

And then, he hadn't had any say in the matter.

They negotiated two more turns, and suddenly were in the cave's twilight zone. Kate had expected to find the same stormy gloom that she had left behind when she entered the cave system. But a brilliant shaft of afternoon sunlight reached in through the entrance.

Kate covered the last dozen or so yards quickly, anxious to remain well ahead of Gavin. On the way out, he had been so eager to lend her a hand at every turn, helping her over uneven ground and through narrow spaces, taking every opportunity to touch her. And every time she felt his strong but gentle grip on her hand, her ankle, her waist, she had felt an almost unbearable ache of belonging.

But his earlier troubled mood had been like a billboard declaring that his feelings for her were deeply conflicted. Putting the man she loved at war with himself . . . well, that made her feel like some kind of interloper. To Kate's way of thinking, love shouldn't make a person feel outside. Love shouldn't cause this kind of pain.

Intent on protecting Gavin's feelings as well as her own, Kate forced herself to put distance between herself and Gavin. With each lengthening step, she warned herself not to allow what she felt for him to turn their relationship into something that either of them might live to regret. And with each step, her heart told her that she was never, ever going to get over Gavin Buckley.

Mark and Zach, side-by-side like two old caving buddies, stepped out through the open gate at the entrance. A sudden babble of voices greeted them, quickly swelling into an excited cheer.

Outside, Kate found a crowd gathered on the muddy ground below the entrance. They were clustered in distinct groups. To the left, half a dozen members of a fire-rescue unit from White Sulphur Springs appeared to have been in the process of donning caving gear. They stood around now in hardhats, looking all dressed up with nowhere to go. They also looked relieved.

Farther down the slope, the Camp Reliant kids, all wearing their first-aid vests, were gathered around Cliff Peet and Toby Harris. Nearby, Mickie Bonner and Lana Peet had maps spread on a makeshift plank table. When Lana glanced up and saw Mark and Zach emerge from the cave, she gave a leap of joy. Mickie pressed a hand to her forehead and looked as if she would like to sit down.

While Mark ambled toward Lana, grinning, Zach drew back his narrow shoulders and headed straight toward Peet.

Zach's camp-mates parted as he approached, gaping at him wide-eyed as if he had suddenly materialized out of thin air. Only Tommy Reyes broke ranks and danced around Zach, crowing, "I thought they'd never find you!"

Zach looked awkward to be the center of such attention. But he stretched a tense smile at Tommy and they exchanged a friendly fist-knock before Zach continued on to where Cliff Peet was waiting.

Man and boy stood three feet apart, eyeing each other as Kate joined them. The boy wore a deep scowl, but it didn't seem to be the chip-on-the-shoulder variety that she had come to know so well.

"Mr. Peet," he said finally in a strong, clear voice, "I shouldn't have gone in the cave all by myself."

"That's right, my boy. You caused a lot of worry."

"Well, I apologize. I won't do it again. And if you'll give me another chance, I promise not to break any more camp rules from now on." He paused long enough to glance at Kate before adding, "You can trust me on that, sir."

Cliff Peet scowled at Zach for a long moment. Then he slowly reached up and rubbed his knobby chin, shifting his gaze to Kate. But she continued to be as astounded as her boss was by Zach's attitude change.

"Well, now," Peet said, studying Zach with deepening interest. "You seem to be a changed man."

Zach didn't blink an eye at being called a man. Kate noticed that the boy had suddenly begun taking a lot of things in stride.

"Miss O'Riley got me to seeing how important it is to be trusted, and to trust in yourself," Zach said.

Peet raised a brow at Kate. "Oh, she did, did she?"

"Yes, sir. And Mr. Buckley . . . well, he kinda showed me how bone-headed it was for me to go snooping around in that cave all by my lonesome."

Peet arched his other brow. "Well, it appears to me that you've been getting all kinds of sage advice."

"The best," Zach said with conviction. "I've learned a lot about risk assessment today."

Off to one side with his arms crossed, Toby caught Kate's eye and gave her a discreet thumbs-up. The other kids had frozen in silence, every eye riveted on Zach. Only Annie Rich pursed her lips, as if waiting for Zach to deliver some kind of punch line.

"In that case, I'll take your situation under advisement," Peet told Zach.

Zack looked at Kate with uncertainty.

She translated, "Mr. Peet will think about it."

The boy looked crestfallen, as if he already knew what decision the camp director would make. Even so, he lifted his chin and said, "Yes, sir."

Peet frowned at the boy for another long while. Then, shaking himself, he said, "Hmmph!" Limping over to the fire-rescue team, he went down the row of men, shaking hands.

"Okay, group, let's get loaded up and back to camp," Toby called out.

The youngsters scurried around gathering up assorted first-aid kits, water jugs, and other supplies. Some appeared disappointed that they hadn't had the opportunity to utilize their equipment and skills.

Kate noticed Mark over with Lana and Mickie. He was pointing at something on the map spread on the makeshift table, and making expansive gestures that Kate could only believe pertained to the newly discovered cavern. Mickie was clearly delighted with what he was describing.

Lana listened to him worshipfully. The three of them were on sloping ground, with Mark standing on the low side, which accentuated his height difference with Lana. But from the rapt way Lana was looking at him, he could have been ten feet tall.

Kate managed a thin smile that quivered at the corners. Love—being loved—had transformed Lana. Kate was happy that Lana had found a man who thought she was worth committing himself to, heart and soul.

Tory headed down the trail toward camp, accompanied by a dozen charges. Kate noticed that Zach brought up the rear as usual, but he had shouldered a double load of water jugs, and there was nothing sullen in his stride.

No matter what decision Cliff Peet chose to hand down, she had a feeling that Zach Forrest would handle it now.

Tears stung the backs of Kate's eyes. She turned away so no one would notice that her emotions were edging out of control, and found herself looking straight at the object of her abiding misery.

Gavin Buckley leaned against the gatepost at the cave entrance, watching her. Kate thought he was probably too far away to see the tears in her eyes. But he seemed to pick up on her emotional high tide all the same, because he looked concerned and took a tentative step toward her. Their gazes met and locked for an eternity.

The departing kids struck up a lively hiking song. Gavin's attention drifted toward the trail just in time to see Zach and Tommy hiking away, both singing along in full voice. When they were gone, his gaze returned to Kate, settling on her like a warm blanket.

He smiled. Was there sadness in his eyes? His lips moved. Kate tried desperately to read them, but she never had been good at that sort of thing.

Finally, he shoved his hands into his pockets and came striding down the slope from the entrance. For a few seconds, it looked as if he was coming to Kate, and her half-broken heart skipped a ragged beat. But at the foot of the slope, Gavin veered off to join the departing fire-rescue workers who were headed up the trail in the opposite direction.

As she watched Gavin leave, Kate's heart squeezed itself down into a hard little knot in her chest. Behind her, she could hear the fading sounds of Zach's voice mingled with the others. Ahead of her, the man she loved more than she would have thought possible walked right out of her life.

Kate tried to console herself with the knowledge that,

where Zach was concerned, she and Gavin had joined forces to accomplish something good and, she hoped, enduring. Finally reaching Zach, saving him from the wilderness into which he'd been thrust by the loss of his father, would be their legacy.

That, she told herself, would have to be enough.

But, oh, she knew it wasn't.

Chapter Ten

Late that evening, Kate sat on the front porch of the main cabin, sipping mugs of spiced tea with Cliff Peet. Lights-out had come to the dorms across the clearing half an hour earlier. Both Lana and Toby had gone off to their rooms shortly thereafter. Kate and her employer were the only two in the compound who were still astir.

And not by much, Kate thought, sagging low in her Adirondack chair. The day had wrung her out, leaving her feeling boneless and lacking in substance. She should have packed it in for the night along with the others. But she knew she would just lie awake dwelling on the image of Gavin Buckley walking out of her life.

"I'll miss these kids," she said with a sigh, trying hard to wrench her thoughts off of what might have been.

"We'll have a new batch on Wednesday," Peet reminded her.

She nodded, though he was staring out toward the dorms and not at her. Maybe by Wednesday, she thought, her spirits would begin to pick up again.

For now, she was preoccupied with how much she

already missed Gavin. It was better that they not see each other again, but it didn't *feel* better yet. What it felt like was the aching empty space left by a recently extracted tooth. She couldn't seem to help probing that emptiness with her heart and mind, yearning for the missing part of her.

Pining for moonmilk and cave pearls.

"Developing a caving program with Borner Enterprises," Peet said, interrupting her thoughts. "That's going to take some work. I'll need someone to manage that part of the operation for me . . . with me."

"Uh-huh," Kate said distractedly.

"I've been thinking, Kate. You've seem to have taken to spelunking like a duck to water. You'd be the perfect person to head this new caving program."

That got her attention. She straightened slowly. "Mr. Peet . . . I don't know what to say." *Much less what to think,* she added to herself.

"Now, I know that's a lot of responsibility," he hurried on, as though afraid she would turn him down before he had a chance to win her over to the idea. "But I can see how having a caving program for our kids could increase attendance several times over. So I'm prepared to offer you a share in Camp Reliant, to make it worth your while."

"A share?" Kate nearly dropped her mug of tea.

She started to tell him that a share in the business wasn't a necessary inducement, and that she would leap at the chance to manage a caving program for the kids if he was convinced she could handle such a challenge. But he didn't give her a chance.

"You have a special way with kids, Kate, and you've turned into a first-rate youth counselor. Now you're probably thinking Toby is senior, so he ought to handle the new caving program. But he already ramrods our wilderness training. And Lana . . . well, Lana and I had a nice long talk last evening. You've made a real impression on that girl, Kate."

Not half the impression that Mark Eisly has made, she wanted to say. But she only smiled.

"Lana is ready to bear down and be the best youth counselor she can," he continued. "But she knows she isn't ready to ramrod anything like a caving program. She's never even been inside a cavern. So Kate, we're all hoping you'll make Camp Reliant a permanent part of your life."

"Of course, I will, Mr. Peet." She was puzzled that he seemed to think she had planned to leave.

"Cliff." He smiled. "If we're going to be partners, call me Cliff."

"Okay." That would take some getting used to. "I'm just so floored that you think I can handle so . . . so much."

He gave her a long, calculating look. "Remember when you came through Camp Reliant as a youngster, Kate?"

She gave a dry laugh. "How could I forget?"

"Well, I told my counselors back then that you had what it took to do anything you dang-well pleased, once you set your mind to it. Now that you're all grown up, you have it within your power to help lead youngsters toward achieving their full potential. You proved that with Zach Forrest."

Kate had never expected to hear such praise from Mr. Peet . . . *Cliff*. She felt flattered, humbled, and more than a little anxious about what lay ahead. But she was excited too. If only—

As if reading her mind, Cliff cleared his throat and

said, "How's it going between you and Gavin Buckley
. . . if you don't mind my asking."

"Nowhere," she said, closing the door on that painful
subject. "It's going nowhere at all."

"That so?" He frowned, looking worried and ready to
poke into the wound that Kate couldn't bear to touch.

She quickly drained her mug and clunked it down onto
the flat wooden arm of her chair. "It's been an incredibly
long day, Mister . . . Cliff. If you don't mind. I'll go run
a final bed-check on the kids, then turn in."

"Sure, Kate." He rose when she did. "You must be
exhausted. I shouldn't have kept you up so late."

"Oh, Cliff." Kate took his callused hand, squeezing it
between both of hers. "You've been so generous. I just
hope I don't do anything to make you regret your confidence in me."

He snorted, still looking concerned and ready to say
something Kate didn't want to hear. So she told him
good night and hurried down off the porch.

Beyond the amber glow of the bug light on the porch,
the clearing was dark. But Kate could have found her
way to the boys' dormitory while blindfolded. She had
made this nocturnal trek nearly every night for the past
six weeks. This was the first night in all that time that
she hadn't approached the dorm with a sense of dread.

At the foot of the dormitory steps, she paused for just
a moment to reflect on the day of changes. She had suffered a broken heart, and gained a career that could make
a positive difference in so many young lives. She wished
she could have had both the man and the work that she
loved. But where Gavin Buckley was concerned, her
luck just hadn't held.

Before sadness over Gavin could drag her spirits into
outright depression, Kate hooked two fingers into the

handle and pulled open the screen door to the dormitory. The spring on the door whined softly as she stepped inside. She stood there for a minute or so, listening—trying to sense whether her hunch was correct.

Then she smiled.

As she moved soundlessly down the center aisle, she was already certain what she would find at the end.

Zach Forrest, sleeping soundly—without so much as a flicker of a nightmare.

Chapter Eleven

At noon on Saturday, Kate sat atop the crossbeam on the rope-net climb, breathing in the mild, sweet-scented breeze. Uphill from this last point on the obstacle course, a portable bleacher had been set up in the shade. The metal bleacher was packed with families of the kids who were now out on the course, running their hearts out for the last honors of the day.

Kate surveyed the fifty or so mothers and fathers, brothers and sisters. Cliff Peet had handed out Camp Reliant T-shirts in pink, yellow, and blue, so the crowd stood out like a festive rainbow against the green of the woods.

Mark and Lana sat at the end of the top bench, holding hands. Down front, Zach Forrest's mother, Rita, looked beside herself with happiness as she watched for her son to appear on the trail. Next to her, looking easily as charged with anticipation as Rita, sat Mickie Bonner.

Farther along that same row sat Mickie's Aunt Lil, whom Kate remembered from her visit to the offices of Bonner Enterprises. The older woman was chatting animatedly with an older man whom Kate took to be Lil's husband, Morgan. Kate couldn't imagine what had brought those two to Camp Reliant that morning.

Mickie smiled radiantly up at Kate and gave her an enthusiastic wave. Gavin's sister had every reason to be excited. Mickie had just solidified an agreement with Cliff Peet to develop a caving program for Camp Reliant's youth. The program would provide beneficial publicity for both Camp Reliant and the caverns when the cave system was opened for tourists.

With a pale smile, Kate waved back. Then she scanned the crowded bleacher one more time, disappointed all over again not to see Gavin. Of course, it was better that he had stayed away. If she had to get over him, better to start now than later.

Mickie gave her another wave—just in case she had missed the first one, Kate guessed. The woman's bouncy exuberance all morning had begun to get on Kate's nerves, curdling her spirits around the edges. Didn't Mickie have a clue that her brother—*twin* brother, for crying out loud—had just broken Kate's heart?

Kate turned back toward the obstacle-course trail, blinking away painful visions of Gavin Buckley.

Cliff Peet had been handing out awards all morning, recognizing everything from first-aid proficiency to wilderness cooking to compass skills. The kids themselves had voted on most of the awards, showing a remarkable degree of fairness. Even Tommy Reyes had been voted the Best Animal Tracker. Only Zach had yet to acquire one of the special certificates of merit for the midsummer program—a fact that didn't seem to dampen Rita Forrest's pride in her son one bit.

Checking her watch again, Kate judged that the lead

runners should be reaching the end of the course within the next minute or so.

She frowned to herself, wondering about the way Zach had performed ever since the morning's activities kicked off at 8:30 sharp. She had an itchy feeling that the boy had been holding himself back. For one thing, she knew with certainty that he was a wizard at building and lighting a campfire without matches. But he had seemed to dog it through the entire demonstration, not getting his fire going until after Tommy's was burning energetically. And Tommy hadn't even gotten the hang of flint-starting a fire until just last week.

The crowd on the bleacher suddenly shot to its feet.

Looking down to her right, Kate spotted two flashes of orange moving in her direction through the trees. Along with everyone on the bleacher, she leaned in that direction, straining to see which participant in the Camp Reliant midsummer program would be first to break into the open.

She knew who she expected that to be: Annie Rich had won just about every footrace she had run at Camp Reliant, on or off the obstacle course. And according to Kate's watch, Annie was about to complete today's run in record time.

The bright orange T-shirts grew closer, weaving through the trees along the trail like a pair of Monarch butterflies. The babble of voices from the bleacher became a steady cheer as the lead runner approached the edge of the trees . . .

. . . and Zach Forrest broke into the clearing.

Kate let out a gasp and almost tumbled off the crossbeam. As she steadied herself, she stole a glance back at the crowd, and saw Mickie Bonner hugging Rita Forrest, both women suddenly ecstatic.

Zach sprinted straight for the obstacle, giving it all he had. The course was a rigorous test of stamina, and Kate could hear his labored panting even over the crowd noise.

He leaped up onto the rope-netting just as Annie Rich entered the clearing. By the time she hit the netting and began her climb, Zach was halfway to the top, moving squirrel-fast despite how much the race had already taken out of him. He grinned at Kate as he neared the crossbeam. After the six weeks that he had spent scuffing along at the tail-end of every group, she could have hugged him for the breakneck effort he was showing.

As he clambered over the crossbeam, Rita Forrest's voice could be heard over the rest. Zach kept grinning, not seeming to mind that his mother was shouting, "My baby! My baby! My baby!" over and over.

Annie Rich's shriek froze everyone in place for a split second.

Then all eyes turned to the girl.

In Annie's haste to catch up with Zach, her foot had slipped through the rope netting midway to the crossbeam. She had lost her grip, and now dangled upside-down, arms flailing the air. With every breath she took, she let out another shriek—part alarm, part outrage.

Kate quickly swung her leg over the crossbeam. But before she could start down the netting to lend Annie a hand, Zach flashed past her. Within seconds, he was at Annie Rich's side.

Annie seemed as astounded as Kate was at the sight of her rescuer. She stopped screaming at once and, with Zach's help, managed to pull herself upright and disentangle her foot.

Since the girl was no longer in danger of injury, Kate followed Camp Reliant policy by resuming her seat on the crossbeam and letting the two work out the difficulty on their own. But she was bursting with pride over the way Zach had sacrificed his lead in order to come to the aid of his stiffest competition.

The two youngsters made such fast work of Annie's predicament that they were once again scrambling up the netting by the time the next runners cleared the edge of the woods. Annie and Zach went over the crossbeam side by side. But this was, for all intents and purposes, Zach's third trip over the obstacle in less than a minute, and he appeared to be totally winded.

Annie Rich beat Zach down the other side by two feet. The sprint to the finish line wasn't even close.

After a slight hesitation, everyone on the bleacher whistled and applauded wildly. Even as Kate turned to supervise the other runners who were just then mounting the obstacle, she could tell the spectators cheering in tribute to more than just Annie Rich's victory. They were also recognizing the selfless action that had cost Zach the race.

The next five runners made it over the obstacle in a bunch, the lead two tying for third place. *Seven down, four to go,* Kate thought, thoroughly enjoying the bird's-eye view of Zach being smothered in his mother's tearful embrace.

Standing next to Rita Forrest, Mickie Bonner smiled up at Kate. On second look, it was more of a knowing little smirk than a smile—one that made Kate uneasy.

Now that Kate thought back, she had been catching Mickie looking at her all through the morning. That the woman had shown up for the final-day events at all had come as a surprise. Usually only family members were interested, though in Mark Eisly's case, romance had proven to be an irresistible draw.

Perhaps Mickie was just trying to get a feel for the kinds of kids who might be participating in future caving programs. That sounded like the only likely reason for the woman's presence. Never the less, she wished Mickie had stayed away, because every time Kate set eyes on her, she was reminded of Gavin.

As another flash of orange appeared through the trees, Kate tried to shake off the latest images of Gavin Buckley. But they clung to the back of her mind, as tenacious as shadows on a sunny day.

The eighth runner broke out into the clearing. For the second time, Kate blinked in disbelief.

"Tom-my!" a husky male voice bellowed from the bleacher as Tommy Reyes ran toward the final obstacle.

Zach wrested free of his mother's embrace and began leaping into the air, joining Tommy's father in shouting his friend's name. Annie added her shrill voice, along with the other youngsters who had already completed the course. Finding their enthusiasm contagious, the entire spectator section took up the chant.

Tommy took hold of the rope-netting and started climbing. He kept his head down, and Kate could hear him repeating a single syllable as he ascended. He was almost to the top before she realized he was saying, "Feet . . . feet . . . feet," reminding himself to watch where he put his feet.

Tommy Reyes had made his choice. Speed was for race horses. He preferred to not make costly mistakes.

"You're number eight, Tommy!" Kate said.

He lifted his head and grinned at her as he swung his leg over the crossbeam. He was crying, tears streaming down his flushed cheeks, so overwhelmed with joy that his teeth were chattering.

"They're all rooting for you," she said, bleary-eyed herself.

"I know," he sobbed. His grin wobbled as he glanced over his shoulder at the bleacher. "I know."

Kate's throat seized up. She watched him ascend the far side of the obstacle, still reminding himself, "Feet . . . feet . . . feet."

The final three runners were climbing the obstacle by the time Tommy reached the ground. Kate quickly turned her attention to them, but she could hear the rousing reception that Tommy received at the finish line. When the last runner had made it over the crossbeam, Kate stole a fleeting glance at the bleacher—just long enough to see Tommy confidently high-fiving his jubilant dad.

The final three hit the ground running. But at the finish line, number nine suddenly stopped short. Number ten skidded to a halt alongside her, as did number eleven, both giving her a quizzical look. They looked at each other for a moment. Then number nine grinned. The others grinned back and threw their arms around each other's shoulders.

Intoning the Camp Reliant motto, "Strength in unity," all four stepped across the finish line together.

Cliff Peet looked flabbergasted as he welcomed them to the end of the race.

After delivering a brief speech on the Camp Reliant spirit, Peet presented Annie Rich with the Obstacle Course Certificate of Excellence. Then, with obvious satisfaction, he handed Zach the coveted red-and-gold Sportsmanship Ribbon.

Zach eyed the ribbon briefly. Then with a smile at his mother, he passed it on to the three contestants who had stepped across the finish line . . . last, but together.

A ripple of applause swept across the bleacher, growing until the spectators came to their feet as one. Without being instructed to, eleven orange T-shirts merged into one tight unit. Kate didn't see a single outsider in the bunch. Every one of her kids looked ready and willing to meet any challenge that life threw at him or her.

Her kids. Kate didn't know when she had begun to think of Camp Reliant's latest batch of kids as hers. But it made her feel as if she too had crossed some kind of finish line, and that she just might be worthy of Cliff Peet's opinion of her.

The only thing missing from that moment was Gavin Buckley. Kate realized that without him, her achievement felt incomplete, like a bird without a song.

The crossbeam quivered slightly as a heavy weight hit the obstacle. Toby Harris sprang up the rope netting, having followed along monitoring the runners through the entire course.

"They turned into a super bunch, didn't they?" he said, joining Kate at the top.

"Remarkable."

"You know, one kid seems to set the tone for each group that passes through camp. Zach Forrest was this session's. When he turned around, they all came together."

"You don't even know how he finished the race," Kate said.

Toby shook his head. "Nope. And it doesn't matter. Today, they all finished first." He scanned the crowd below. "They all have you to thank for that, Kate."

"Me?" He had to be kidding.

"Yes, you. Didn't Mr. Peet tell you? The kids voted you the counselor who influenced them the most."

"Me?" she repeated.

That news, on top of Cliff Peet's business offer the

night before, was too much to absorb. Kate began to feel herself lose touch with reality.

"It was unanimous." Toby laughed, delighted that he'd managed to totally fluster her. "Tell ya what, Kate—Mr. Peet, Lana, and I are *jealous*."

He started down the netting. Kate moved to descend with him, but Toby held up a hand like a school-crossing guard.

"Better stay put, Kate, just in case there are any stragglers still out on the course."

"What are you talking about? All eleven kids are present and accounted for."

"Sit tight." Suddenly stern, Toby pointed a finger at her. "That's an order."

Kate might have become a junior partner in Camp Reliant the previous night, but the rules of that arrangement were yet to be made clear to her. As far as she knew, Toby was still senior counselor. She settled back onto the beam, nonplused. Toby had never blatantly pulled rank on her like that before. And why now? For heaven's sake, she could count. There were no more kids on the trail.

The crowd was filing down off the bleacher, preparing to head off toward the camp compound. But Cliff Peet made no move in that direction; nor did Toby, Mickie Bonner, Lana Peet, or Mark Eisly. All of those had taken seats on the front row of the bleacher, as though awaiting the second feature at a movie theater.

When the rest of the crowd noticed this, they came straggling back onto the bleacher. Some of them looked embarrassed, clearly assuming that they had prematurely left their seats before the event had officially ended.

Kate stared down from her perch, wondering what was going on. The final-day schedule of events didn't call for further activities at the obstacle course. According to the leaflet handed out to family members, they should be gathering at the compound for a big barbecue lunch. She could even smell hickory smoke from the barbecue pit wafting on the breeze.

Her stomach rumbled.

Then the crossbeam quivered again.

Startled, Kate looked down . . . and sucked in a strangled breath.

Gavin Buckley was on the rope-netting. He climbed slowly, his gaze locked with hers as intently as a cat stalking its prey, a bright flame burning in the depths of his eyes. His lips were set in a hard line. Everything about him spoke of an underlying tension wound tight, just short of the snapping point.

At the top, he straddled the crossbeam, facing Kate. They just stared at each other for a long moment, drinking deeply. Kate's pulse had quickened to a gallop, even as her confusion spun utterly out of control.

"Gavin, what are you—"

He raised a finger and made a shushing sound. Kate fell silent. He wiped both hands down the front of his shirt and flexed his fingers.

Tension release, she thought. *He's . . . scared.* The very idea that Gavin Buckley was frightened alarmed her no end.

"Kate O'Riley," he said in a loud voice that carried over the clearing, "I've made my share of dumb moves in my life, but by far the stupidest was telling you I had doubts about marriage."

She gaped at him, stunned. That made Gavin smile, just a little, like the stretching of an already taut banjo string. Gavin dug into the key pocket of his shorts and came up with a ring. He turned it slowly in front of her face, making the diamond glint in the sunlight.

"I love you, Kate. In fact, love seems like too small a word to describe how I feel about you." He paused, licked his lips, and then seemed to suck in courage through his teeth.

Kate continued to stare at him in disbelief. Just a moment ago, she had feared that she might never see him again. And now . . . now . . .

His next words carried like a velvet thunderbolt across the clearing. "Katie," he said with only the slightest quaver of tension in his voice, "will you make me the happiest man in the world by taking me as your husband?"

Kate's vision blurred briefly. She opened her mouth. No sound came out. She tried again with similar result.

Gavin leaned closer, looking pale beneath his summer tan. "Say something, my love," he said in an undertone, "or I swear I'll kiss you right here in front of an audience of thousands."

She flushed, belatedly remembering the crowd on the bleacher. But she couldn't make herself look down for even a second, not while the most amazing experience of her life was taking place right up there on the crossbeam.

"Fifty," she heard herself say. "An audience of fifty."

He arched a brow, and then smiled again, this time warmly. "Yes, sweetheart. But just think how many people they're going to tell about this. Why, Mickie alone has a grapevine the size of—"

"I will," Kate cut in.

His lips parted. He went perfectly still for several seconds, too overwhelmed by her acceptance to take his next breath. Or perhaps, like Kate, he was simply savoring the two words that had the power to change their lives forever.

"Louder," he whispered hoarsely, taking her left hand in his. "Say it loud enough for those in the cheap seats to hear."

"Gavin Buckley," Kate said, feeling the engagement ring slip onto her finger—a perfect fit, "*I will.*"

From below came Tommy's high, clear, "Go-ooo, Miss O'Riley!"

That was seconded by Zach's, "Go-ooo, Mr. Buckley!"

Grinning at the enthusiastic cheering section, Gavin never took his gaze off Kate's eyes as he raised her hand and pressed the ring to his lips. Then he leaned into a long, warm kiss. Kate's lips seemed to melt into his, and the roar in her ears drowned out the celebratory commotion that had erupted in the bleacher.

They finally got around to climbing down from the crossbeam. On solid ground, Kate's knees wobbled as if she had been out to sea for a long time and had lost her land legs. Still in a daze, she endured a dreamlike flurry of hugs and congratulations. Mickie Bonner's beaming face stood out among the rest as she stepped forward to embrace Kate as a sister.

And then Kate was left blissfully alone with Gavin as the festive mob moved off toward the compound. Gavin tucked her under his arm and they followed the others at a slower pace, taking their time.

"I can't believe what just happened," Kate said, still breathless. She suddenly felt acutely attuned to her surroundings—the smell of pine needles and damp woodland humus—the loud, clear song of a yellow-throated warbler—the glint of the midday sun through the tree branches—the solid, treelike solidity of Gavin next to her, and the sense that he would always be there no matter what. "I just cannot believe it."

He made a growling sound. "That had to have been the most terrifying moment of my life, bar none."

She stopped and turned to face him. "Then why did you make it so . . . public? Wouldn't it have been easier for you to propose . . ." She fished around for a more conventional setting ". . . over dinner?"

"Oh, yes." He gently fingered a wisp of hair from her eyes. "It would have been a lot easier, especially if you'd had the good sense to turn me down. And believe me, after the way I've bad-mouthed marriage, you'd have had every right to tell me to take a hike. But I wanted you to know just how much I was willing to risk—total humiliation, if necessary—in order to win the privilege of being a permanent part of your life."

Kate threw her arms around him. They held each other, rocking slightly in the pungent breeze. She closed her eyes, marveling at all the magic that Gavin had brought into her life.

Mighty Ursa Major, the Great Bear, striding across the night sky.

Glittering silent cathedrals with still pools of moon milk.

Cave pearls.

"Oh!" Her eyes popped open as she remembered. She had all but forgotten her little oversight. But it was one she intended to remedy before the weekend was over.

Epilogue

Kate kept her eyes clamped shut as instructed.

In the silence of the cavern, she could hear her heartbeat in her ears, rapid with excitement. Her pulse quickened when she was around Gavin. She had a feeling that it would always be that way, even after they had grown old and gray together.

Somewhere off to her left came another faint spitting sound, like and angry cat or the flick of a lighter. She smiled, tempted to peek. But she had given her word not to, so she remained statue-still on the flat rock where Gavin had seated her, trying to keep a tight rein on her curiosity.

They were in *their* cavern, as Kate thought of it—the one that Gavin had brought her to on her first trip into the mountain. Before they entered the room, he'd extinguished their lanterns, using a small flashlight with a pinpoint beam to lead her to the rock. Ever since, she had been waiting there with her eyes closed.

With the midsummer program ended, Camp Reliant was deserted that Sunday. When Gavin and Mark had

arrived at the compound at 2:00 in the afternoon, Kate
and Lana were the only people on the premises. As Kate
stepped out onto the porch to greet the two men, Mark
had bolted straight past her into the main cabin in search
of his lady love.

Gavin had come bounding up the steps, thrown down
a large sack identical to the one that Mark had carried
inside, and swept Kate off her feet. He swung her around
in a roaring bear hug that left her laughing with delight.
After a lingering kiss, he had picked up the bag and
handed it to her. Inside, Kate had found her very own
canary-yellow jumpsuit and matching hardhat.

She wore both now, sitting there on the rock.

Even after their long trek into the cave system, the
jumpsuit felt new—just like the ring on her finger, and
the new life that was opening up for her.

"Hey, there." Gavin spoke softly as he eased down
next to her. "What are you smiling about?"

"I'm happy, Gav. I didn't know it was possible to be
this happy."

"Gosh. If I'd known a new hardhat would do that for
you, I'd have gotten you one right off."

She elbowed him playfully, and then snuggled blissfully close as he put an arm around her. "May I open
my eyes now? Or do I have to wait until Mark and Lana
get here?"

"They aren't coming. Mark is taking her to the bigger
cavern that Zach found Friday. We'll meet them there in
an hour."

"Whoa!" Kate smiled again. "There's nothing like
starting Lana with the main event on her first trip into
the mountain."

"Uh-huh. By the end of the day, Mark plans to have
her totally sold on caving."

Kate nudged him. "You two are devious, luring unsuspecting women with your fantastic Cinderella castles."

"Oh, yeah?" With a chuckle, Gavin reached down and tapped her hiking boots. "I'll remember to bring the glass slipper next time."

He smothered her laughter with a kiss that made Kate dizzy, and then he drew away. After stroking her cheek with a finger, he murmured, "You can open your eyes now."

Kate hesitated, wishing for another kiss. Then, half-reluctantly, she opened her lids.

She was facing Gavin, so the first thing she saw was a thousand fireflies dancing in his eyes. At least, that's what the tiny golden glints reminded her of until she realized they were candlelight.

Kate turned her head toward the source of light. Her eyes widened, and her hand drifted to her mouth in awe.

They were sitting in front of the moonmilk pool in which they had accidentally bathed last week—an incident that seemed to have taken place forever ago. Gavin had placed a dozen or so collapsible lanterns along the edge of the rimstone border of the pool. The wavering candlelight reflected off the opaque water, shimmering like a dream.

"Oh, Gav," she sighed, "it's beautiful. Like a magic mirror." If she stared at it long enough, Kate thought, surely she would see the face of a genie.

"I hoped you'd like it. And I hope you like the rest."

Kate pried her gaze from the pool and looked at him. "The rest?"

He took her hands. "I'm moving down here permanently to help Mickie develop the caves for tourists. It'll be a major job, and she'll need all the help she can get."

Gavin smiled. "And guess what she's giving us for a wedding present?"

She could only shake her head, astounded by the news that Gavin was giving up his professorship in Pennsylvania to move to these mountains.

"Mickie's giving us this room." His sweeping gesture took in their cavern, with its soaring calcite columns, surreal stalactites, and scattered pools of moonmilk. "We can develop it for your kids' program."

We. Her heart swelled at the sound of that. Kate threw her arms around Gavin, overwhelmed by Mickie's incredible generosity.

They talked happily about their plans for a while, and then simply stared at the candlelit moonmilk as if mesmerized by its ancient magic. After what seemed like a very short time, Gavin sighed.

"We'd better get moving," he said. "It's about time to meet Mark and Lana over in the big cavern." He started to get up.

"Wait." Kate dug into a pocket of her jumpsuit. She came up with a small tissue, which she carefully unfolded to reveal a perfect cave pearl. "This is the one that got stuck in my shorts during our moonmilk dunking."

"Ah." Gavin fingered the pearl. "The little hitchhiker."

"Yes. A little hitchhiker who's going home."

She leaned over and dipped her hand lightly into the pool. The pearl rolled off her palm into the moonmilk. As it sank out of sight, Kate felt it bind her to the cavern, just as the cavern had bound her to the man she loved.

"Let's go," she whispered. *We have dreams to keep.*